Death and Donuts

A BEE'S BAKERY COZY MYSTERY BOOK 1

ROSIE A. POINT

Death and Donuts
A Bee's Bakery Cozy Mystery Book 1

Cover by DLR Cover Designs
www.dlrcoverdesigns.com

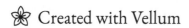 Created with Vellum

You're invited!

Hi there, reader!

I'd like to formally invite you to join my awe-
some community of readers. We love to chat
about cozy mysteries, cooking, and pets.

It's super fun because I get to share chapters
from yet-to-be-released books, fun recipes, pictures, and do giveaways with the people who
enjoy my stories the most.

So whether you're a new reader or you've been
enjoying my stories for a while, you can catch up

with other like-minded readers, and get lots of cool content by visiting my website at *www.rosie-pointbooks.com* and signing up for my mailing list.

Or simply search for me on *www.bookbub.com* and follow me there.

I look forward to getting to know you better.

Let's get into the story!

Yours,
Rosie

One

"I'm telling you, Bee," I said, my heart thrumming against my throat, "it's gone."

"Gone?" Her voice whipped through the phone, commanding and straight to the point as ever. Our move from the traveling food truck that had been our home away from home to Mystery, Maine, and a brick and mortar bakery, had changed our lives forever.

But not Bee's personality. She was just as boisterous, in control, and blunt. A constant that I needed when life got complicated.

"Ruby? Are you there? What do you mean, it's gone? Have you told Jamie about this?"

"I—Not yet. It was there this morning." I pressed my thumb to the inside of my ring finger, staring at the closed glass front door of the bakery. "I must have dropped it somewhere. But I'm not sure where? I'm trying to retrace my steps but—"

"Don't panic, Rubes," Bee said briskly. "Whatever happens, you'll handle it. Make sure you check under the counter. And maybe between the cakes on display? I'll be back from the bank in fifteen minutes. I'll help you find it."

"Thanks, Bee."

"What are friends for?" And then she hung up, and I was alone in our fabulous bakery without my engagement ring.

It was the weirdest thing, but over the past week, it had gone missing about five times. It was a brand new ring that Jamie had bought from the jewelry store right next door to the bakery. And when I'd tried it on, it had fit perfectly. So why did it keep falling off?

Heavens, it wasn't like I'd been dipping my fingers in butter or something. Bee did all the baking, and I managed the front of house in our new bakery.

My mood lifted at the thought.

We had moved to the quaint, seaside town of Mystery, Maine, over two months ago and opened our bakery, Bee's Bakery, soon after. What was the sense in waiting? Bee had always wanted a little place of her own, and I needed the distraction from the wedding planning. And the self-doubt.

Moving to a new town and settling down had been challenging for me. And I couldn't help but second-guess every decision I made, whether it was to do with the bakery or the wedding.

"I should get hold of Moira," I muttered under my breath. Moira was my wedding planner—she'd been a great help in relieving the stress of finding everything myself. And with Jamie looking for work—

"Were you talking to yourself?" A throaty voice, deep as a donut hole, drifted across the room.

The bakery had just opened, and we'd had about two customers so far this morning—the steady flow of townsfolk in search of baked goods and delicious sweet treats would start soon enough.

A man stood just inside the glass front door. He wore a crooked smile that matched the fit of his clothing. A thatch of curly hair sat tight against his scalp, and he took a tentative step toward me, giving the impression of a turtle sticking its head out of its shell.

"Hello," I said, putting up my most welcoming smile, though he had the strangest manner. "How are you?"

"On the list of cardinal sins, gluttony should be nearer the top," he said, stopping after another higgledy-piggledy step, slow-footed, sure, and entirely disconcerting.

Don't be mean, Ruby. You don't know this man. Sure, he seems creepy but that might be because it's fall. Halloween's around the corner.

He was both withdrawn and too tall for the interior of the bakery. His presence didn't quite gel with the honeycomb decorations, the mural of bees and honey on the wall, the golden-walnut flooring, or the merry yellow booth chairs. Our interior decorator—Bee—had taken the theme "Bee's Bakery" quite literally. The bakery was decorated in golds, creams, yellows, and rich earthy colors.

A silence drifted between us. The morning rush in the bakery would start soon, but, for now, it was just him and me in here and our assistant chef, Leslie, in the kitchen.

"My name's Ruby," I said, blowing past the odd comment. "And you are?"

"Gluttony," he continued, "is a sin. But I s'pose you get that a lot."

He had a faint Northeastern accent, but it was mixed with something else I couldn't place.

"Are you interested in a coffee?" I asked. "Or a donut? We've got a brilliant new flavor that—"

He sidled forward and stopped in front of the counter. I fiddled with my empty ring finger, trying not to draw back from his presence. This town had plenty of interesting inhabitants, but they were mostly friendly and welcoming, though many of the folks we'd met had an enigmatic quality about them. Maybe that was why they'd chosen to live in Mystery in the first place.

"Do you know what else is a sin?" he asked, shrewdly, keeping my gaze. He was much taller up close.

5

"Uh—"

"Theft." He opened his palm and held it out.

My ring sat against his skin.

"That's mine," I said, reaching for it. "Where did you find it?" The strange man allowed me to pluck it from his palm, and I hurriedly slid it into place on my ring finger with a grateful sigh. "Thank you."

"You should be more careful with your things."

"How did you know it was mine?" If the past few years had taught me anything it was that an inquisitive mind was always rewarded. Gosh, where had this guy come from? And why was he talking about sins and—?

"I heard you talking on the phone." He lifted his thumb and pinky finger to his ear. "And the ring was on the sidewalk out front."

"Thank you so much. I've been looking for it everywhere."

"Except the sidewalk out front," he replied.

I opened my mouth, summoning up an equally snarky retort, but the kitchen door swung open and Leslie emerged from within, her dark hair threatening to escape from under her chef's hat. "Ruby," she said. "The bread dough for the bread pudding."

"What about it?" Silent dread descended on me. The darn bread dough always flopped when Bee was out of the bakery. It was the one thing I was *terrible* at fixing.

"It's happened again. I don't know what's wrong with me," Leslie said, "but I can't get it right. It's like I'm cursed." She lifted her fingers and twiddled them at me. "Can you help me, please?"

"Sure," I said, "I'll be right in. I'm just with a customer."

Leslie's dark forehead wrinkled. "Customer?"

"Yeah, he was about to order—" I turned, gesturing to the stranger and found the interior of the bakery was completely empty. "What on earth? I swear, he was just here. He gave me my ring." I lifted my finger, showing off the ring. "And he was talking about gluttony and—"

Leslie shut one eye and widened the other, giving me a look. "I might not be the only one who's cursed."

7

"Very funny," I said.

Leslie had been working with us for a month —she was a qualified but inexperienced pastry chef, kind, funny, and often sarcastic, she had quickly become our friend. "Seriously, though. The bread dough?"

"Where is bread pudding from, anyway?" I asked.

"The United Kingdom, I think." Leslie massaged the air with her fingers. "Help."

"Coming, coming." I spared a glance for the bakery interior, scanning the empty tables, the closed front door, and the sunny street outside. Where had the man come from?

And more importantly, where had he gone?

Two

THE BREAD DOUGH WAS SOMETHING TO behold.

Leslie and I stood side-by-side between the polished silver countertops, the state-of-the-art oven, and the many implements that were kept neat, clean and orderly, staring into the depths of the silver bowl.

"See what I mean?" Leslie poked the offending dough with a finger. It made an unattractive *plop* of noise that sounded a little too close to a burp for my liking. "It's done. Gone. It doesn't matter how I approach it, or what I do, it always ends up like this."

"It's kind of..." I searched for the right words.

"Gross?"

"I was going to say unappealing."

"So, gross."

"It has personality," I said. "That's something at least."

"I prefer my dough without the personality," Leslie said. "I have enough of it to go around."

"You do." I tilted my head.

"I studied how to make this stuff in college," Leslie said, despondent, "and I got it right every time. I can't figure out why it flops whenever I try to make it over the past couple of weeks."

"The curse," I whispered, "of the floppy dough."

Leslie prodded it again, and it burped in response. "Flatulent."

"That's a much better word."

"My bread dough is gross and flatulent," Leslie said, pulling a face. "I've failed you and Bee."

"Nonsense. You're a great chef. And it's been a pleasure having you here. You know how Bee feels about waking up early," I said.

"But the bread pudding..."

"It's more of a donut day anyway." I gave her shoulder a gentle squeeze. "Don't worry about it."

Leslie shivered. "Is it just me, or is it cold in here?"

The door swung open, and Bee entered the kitchen. Her hazel eyes were bright with excitement, and she flashed me her signature gap-toothed grin. "What's going on? Did you find the ring?"

I lifted my finger to show it off, diamond and all. "I found it," I said, "but I—"

Bee gasped at the sight of the dough. "What in the—?"

"I tried," Leslie said mournfully. "But I can't get it to work. It's like it's got a vendetta against me. It's like it can sense my fear."

Bee poked it, and for a third and final time, the dough let out a fantastic *toot*. "How rude. What an objectionable piece of work." Bee grabbed her apron—striped black and yellow like a bee—from behind the door and put it on hurriedly, tying it around her trim waist. "We'll start again."

Leslie let out a sigh. "You're not mad?"

"Of course not," Bee said. "Bread dough has always been the nemesis of an experienced baker. Just throw it out, and let's get this show on the road." She'd already slipped a hairnet over her silver-gray locks.

Leslie stood beside Bee as she started a fresh batch of pastry, taking note of every move and measurement she made. I admired them, working together, so in sync and enjoying the baking in a way I never could.

"So, Ruby," Bee said. "You found the ring. How? Where?"

I pressed my thumb to it, checking it was there. "It's a weird story, actually."

"You know how much I love those."

I told her about the stranger who had come in talking about gluttony and theft before promptly presenting me with the ring.

"That *is* weird," Bee said. "Wish I'd been here to see him. He doesn't sound familiar. Do you know the guy, Leslie?"

"His description doesn't match anyone I know from around Mystery"

"Hmm." Bee looked ready to scratch her

chin, but her hands were full of flour. "But you say he was strange?"

"Beyond strange," I replied. "He kind of gave me the creeps. But then, I thought maybe I was being too harsh."

"You always were a bleeding heart," Bee said. "You know what I would've done if a creepy man had come through the door talking about gluttony?"

"Pelted him with donuts?"

"Right on the money." Bee pointed a finger gun at me, and a bit of dough dropped from her fingertip back into the bowl. "That's the thing, Ruby, when you get that vibe, that strange atmosphere from someone or something, you've got to trust your gut."

I nodded.

Bee's brow wrinkled. "You used to be great at that. You can't be a successful investigative reporter without trusting your gut."

"Who said I was successful?"

Bee snorted.

"You were an investigative journalist?" Leslie asked.

"Back in ye old yesteryear," I replied. "When I still had the knack for it."

"You do still have the knack for it." Bee was always my greatest cheerleader.

I didn't comment. We'd been through so many changes lately, and then there was the fact that I'd started living with Jamie. Sure, we still slept in separate bedrooms—all the way up until we get married—but it was different.

Life had gone from traveling and exploring to settling down in Mystery, and I was trying to regain that old sense of myself that I'd had in the past.

Better not to trust my gut when I could barely get my affairs or thoughts in order.

"After we're done here," Bee said, "we can pop next door to the jewelry store and have them resize your ring. They have to do it after the number of times it's gone missing this week."

I nodded. I hadn't told Jamie about the ring issue. I didn't want him to think I didn't have things under control. "That would be great."

A pleasant silence drifted through the kitchen.

"So, how's the job hunt going?" Bee cheerfully changed the subject as she worked on the dough under Leslie's watchful eye.

"Job hunt? Oh, you mean for Jamie? Fine, I think," I said. "He's going to apply for a job at the local police station. I don't know how that's going to work given everything, but we'll see."

"Why does he want to work?" Leslie asked.

Both Bee and I looked over at her.

"Sorry," she said with a sheepish grin. "I was curious. I know that he's probably the richest guy in town. There are rumors spinning out of control in Mystery. Most people don't get why a millionaire would want a *normal* job."

"To be a part of the community," Bee said. "It's good to be a part of something bigger than oneself."

Or maybe it's to get away from me. I kept the silly, negative thought to myself. Mystery was a lovely town. *Of course* Jamie wanted to find a job here, be a part of the community, and contribute to the—

"Hello!" A gruff voice called from the bakery proper. A customer had arrived. "Hey! Anybody in here?"

"Coming," I called, excusing myself from

the kitchen. I entered the dining area to find the local detective—an older gentleman who re-minded me of a grizzly bear except for the silver hair and pink cheeks—standing in front of the counter.

"About darn time," he said. "My stomach's chewing a hole through my shirt."

I put up a smile, trying to press my worries aside and focus on the here and now. So far, Mystery had been nothing but pleasant. I had to put my sense of foreboding aside. Nothing bad was going to happen in this town. It was our home now.

Three

AFTER THE BREAD DOUGH DISASTER HAD been averted and the morning rush had slowed to a crawl, Bee popped her head out of the kitchen doorway and gave me "the look."

Bee's "look" always had a similar underlying message—time to get your butt into gear—and applied to many situations, whether it was to do with investigating a murder or making sure I took time for myself instead of working myself to the bone.

"What did I do?" I asked.

Bee snorted. "Let's get that ring resized.

Leslie will pop out of the kitchen for a while and make sure the customers are looked after."

I stripped off my apron and hung it on the peg behind the counter. "That reminds me," I said. "I need to hire someone else to handle the front of house once things are in full swing."

"We're swinging pretty well," Bee said, heading over to the coat stand to grab her trench coat. I grabbed my scarf and put it on, smiling at her enthusiasm.

She wasn't wrong. Things were going well at Bee's Bakery. The locals trusted us, and we sold out of cakes and treats often, but it was still a work in progress. Things could always be better.

I followed Bee out into the street and shivered in the cool morning breeze. Fall was here all right. The trees that towered in sidewalk beds had shed many of their leaves. The oranges, golds, reds, and browns littering the street gave me a sense of inner comfort.

Bee and I hurried to the jewelry store next door, entering the gated enclosure that separated the street from the interior.

Bee pressed a button beside the gate. A

second later, a buzz and a clack followed and we were permitted entry.

The owner of the store leaned over the counter, examining a piece of jewelry closely. His dark hair, flecked gray, fell loose around his shoulders as he worked, his fingers sure and precise. "A fine day for coats and bats," he said, without looking up.

"Bats?" I asked.

A smirk lifted his cheeks, and he finally looked up at us. "It's almost Halloween." He didn't have a "north-eastern" accent.

This was my first time meeting him, and he kind of gave me the creeps. Then again, everybody had been giving me the creeps lately. Maybe it was just a creepy time of year. "I'm Ruby," I said.

"I know who you are."

See? That's creepy!

Bee arched a silver eyebrow. "Great," she said, "but who are you?"

He set aside the jewelry piece he'd been examining in a velvet tray then leaned both palms on the countertop. He had dexterous fingers, long and pale. "Marcus Baron," he said. "Owner of this establishment. You're the bakers from next-door—I've seen you around."

This was the elusive Mr. Baron? We'd sent him an email invite to the launch of the bakery months ago, and he'd politely declined. Via snail mail! With a thick wax stamp on the back of the envelope.

But other than that, he'd been a surprisingly good neighbor. There'd been no arguments between us or noise complaints or anything at all. Just silence.

"Nice to finally meet you," Bee said.

"Finally," Mr. Baron agreed. "I was hoping you'd pop by at some point, but then I prefer my quiet times. I'm not always here."

"Oh," I said, because I wasn't sure what else to say after that declaration.

The tinkle of classical music from the speakers in the corners filled the quiet. The glass cases stocked with jewelry pieces on velvet backing watched us struggle through the awkward encounter. I scuffed my foot on the thick red carpeting underfoot.

"I came to get my ring resized," I said, lifting my hand. "It keeps falling off."

"Oh? And it's one of ours?"

"Yes, sir," I said. "I believe my fiancé purchased it from a Mr. Cody?"

"Just Cody," Mr. Baron said. "No 'mister' required." He leaned back and let out a quick sharp whistle through his two front teeth. "He'll be with you in a moment, but bring the ring over here and let me have a look."

"Sure." I approached the desk and started removing the ring.

Mr. Baron caught my hand before I could, examining the fit. "Did your fiancé bring the correct ring size?"

"Yes," I said. "I had a ring before this one, but he wanted something specially made."

"That's not like Cody," Mr. Baron murmured. I got the impression he was disturbed by the mistake from more than a business perspective. "Yeah, this doesn't fit at all." He slipped the ring from my finger without asking and placed it on the glass countertop. A stray beam of sunlight caught the diamond set in its platinum band and rainbow colors refracted from the stone.

The door to a back room opened, and Cody —I assumed it was him—emerged. Short and tanned, he cast a harried glance at his boss and squirreled over to the counter. "What's wrong?"

"The size is incorrect," Mr. Baron said. "Custom-made yet incorrect. Strange, Cody. Very strange."

"I'll look into it. I—"

"Boom, Boom, Boom, Boom!" by the Venga Boys cut across his words, and Mr. Baron hurriedly rifled through his pockets and produced his cellphone. "I've got to take this," he said. "It's my son. Cody, make this better, all right?"

"Yes, boss."

Mr. Baron headed for the door to the back room, his phone already pressed to his ear. "Noel, I've told you not to call me during work. If you're not going to help, then you can have the decency to..." The door shut behind him.

Bee recovered from the strange interlude faster than me. "Interesting choice of ringtone for that man."

"A gothic symphony would probably have suited him better," I agreed.

Bee grinned at me. "Snarky in your old age."

"I don't mean to be."

"Don't look so guilty," Bee replied. "Snark is the sauce of life." She turned to Cody, and he paled beneath her fierce gaze. Bee was great at shriveling men and women alike when they got in her way. "I don't think it's fair that Ruby should have to pay for a resizing. You were given the correct size for her ring, weren't you?"

"It's OK, Bee—"

"No, it's not OK," Bee said. "You can't let people take you for a ride. Not when they've promised you something. Heck, not ever."

Cody patted the air, casting nervous glances left and right. "Don't worry about money. It was my mistake." He considered the ring, if only to escape Bee's vicious glare. "I can have this resized for you in two weeks."

"Two weeks!" Bee gasped.

"Yes," Cody said. "I'm afraid that's how long it takes."

The wedding was in two months. And while two weeks without an engagement ring wasn't that bad, it was still cutting it pretty close to the time we'd get married. *That's silly. You don't need an engagement ring to get married.*

"Thank you," I said, cutting Bee off before she could fuss anymore. I didn't need her stressing on top of everything else. Heavens, I had a meeting with my wedding planner later on, and that was more than enough cortisol for one day.

"Are you sure about this, Ruby?" Bee squeezed my arm. "You could just get a ring from somewhere else. I'm sure Jamie would take the refund and—"

"It's fine," I said. "I like to support local businesses." And not having the engagement ring to worry about was kind of nice. Not in an emotional or "cold feet" way, but in a "it's not falling off my finger every five seconds" way.

I let out a sigh, exhaling my worries as best I could. "Thank you, Cody," I said.

He gave a nervous nod.

Bee and I exited the jewelry store to the buzz and clang of the gate behind us. So far, the week had started off strange, but things would get better soon. The minute the stress of the wedding was gone, my fears and self-doubt and everything in between would dissipate too.

Mystery was a beautiful town. It was my home now. I'd learn to accept that, no matter how *weird* things got.

Four

Later that night...

WITH A NEW TOWN CAME NEW FAMILY traditions. The word "family" had a nice ring to it, and now I had one. I had Jamie and Bee, and our nightly dinners that often ran late. Bee didn't like to wake up early, but she enjoyed the occasional glass of red wine with dinner and chatting at our worn antique table in the dining room.

Our house—a double story clapboard affair

—was sequestered between trees at the end of a long dirt path and had taken a lot of love and care to get into shape. Thankfully, Jamie had the funds to help us do exactly that.

Homemaking hadn't been on my list of priorities, and I felt privileged to have a wealthy fiancé who cared enough to make me comfortable. And Bee too. He'd purchased a property with a cottage for her to live in.

"Maine Lobster Lasagna," Jamie said, pride radiating from the words. He set down a gorgeous ceramic dish on the potholder in the center of our table.

The smell of melted cheese and Alfredo sauce drifted from the dish, and my mouth watered. Jamie had a real passion for cooking, and he'd been trying out new recipes ever since we'd arrived in Mystery.

Seriously, could he get more perfect. He was expressive, handsome as they came, with blond hair and bright eyes, and he loved to cook.

Why on earth would he want to marry me? I forced the errant thought aside. I'd been having more of them of late, and they weren't helpful.

I smiled up at my gorgeous fiancé. "Smells delicious."

Bee entered the dining area, phone in hand and stared at the dish on the table. "You've outdone yourself yet again, Hanson."

"Thank you, Pine," he replied. "Now, take a seat before it gets cold."

"Bossy." Bee set down her phone and joined us at the table. A warmth traveled through my chest at having her here with us.

If I'd pictured my life a few years ago, I'd never have guessed that we'd be here now. Together. Or that Bee or Jamie would even have been a part of it. And the murders? Well, the murder cases we'd solved had been bittersweet.

"Lasagna?" Bee moved to the edge of her chair.

"Lobster Lasagna," Jamie corrected. "I got the recipe from the chef at The Claw Pot, that place I wanted us to try?"

"You two are due a date night," Bee said. "I'm always here cramping your style."

"You could never cramp our style." I smiled at her.

Jamie agreed before slicing into the lasagna.

He dished it neatly into plates for us, and my stomach growled. It was past 08:00 p.m. and I hadn't had a bite to eat since this afternoon. Did donuts really count anymore?

He'd paired the delicious lasagna with a fresh green salad with balsamic dressing. I lost myself in the delicate flavors and cheesy goodness.

"Jamie, this is outstanding," Bee said. "I don't know how you do it."

"I'm glad you're enjoying it," he replied.

And that was when I noticed it. Jamie hadn't had a bite to eat since we'd sat down. His slice of lasagna sat cooling in its dish.

"What's wrong?" I reached across the table and squeezed his hand.

He gave me an easy smile in response and squeezed back. "Nothing's wrong. I guess that's a white lie. I'm nervous." Jamie laughed.

"Nervous?" Bee asked, forkful of lasagna halfway to her mouth. "Why? What have you done? Whose body do we have to bury?"

"Bee!"

"You're right," Bee said, and ate her bite of food with a flourish of her fork. "We'd never bury a body, only find the murder, and if you're

29

the culprit, Hanson, you have every right to be nervous."

"I appreciate the vote of confidence," Jamie said, rising from the table, "but this has nothing to do with dead bodies."

"Thank goodness." I massaged my chest. We'd dealt with enough murder cases to last us a lifetime. Or at least a moderately successful detective's career.

"Then what's going on?" Bee asked. "Or as the kids say 'cracka-lackin.'"

"I'm not an expert on colloquialisms," I said, "but I'm pretty sure the kids don't say that anymore. Or ever."

Bee shrugged.

Jamie rose from the table without a word and exited the dining area and its en suite kitchen—gleaming white tiles, cream walls, and a view of the woods out back.

"Jamie?" I called.

Silence.

"He's got a flair for the dramatic," Bee said. "I always suspected it, but now it's confirmed. Then again, most men do. They like to think they're all down-to-earth, but most men gossip worse than women I've met."

She wasn't wrong. We'd encountered plenty of men in our travels who had no qualms about spilling the baking beans.

A moment passed.

Jamie returned, holding a cardboard box with no lid.

"Do I want to know what's in there?" Bee asked.

"Is it the Halloween decor I asked you to get?" I clapped my hands.

"Nope." Jamie set the box down on the table next to the lasagna. "It's Cookie."

"Cookies?" Bee asked. "Anticlimactic given our line of work."

"No," Jamie laughed. "Not cookies. Cookie. Cookie your new pet cat."

Bee and I both gasped and clasped our hands together, mirrors of excitement. It was the one thing we'd always missed when we'd been on the road. We'd never had a pet, and we'd dreamed of it. Bee and I both loved cats and dogs.

We scraped our chairs backward and peered into the box.

A ginger kitten with a cute furry white chest and pretty green eyes sat purring in the box. Its paws were planted neatly in front of its fluffy body, and I got the impression that it was intelligent and keen to meet us.

"Hello, Cookie. Where are you from?" Bee cooed, and put out a hand.

The kitten purred and rubbed the side of its head against her palm.

"Adorable," I said. "Jamie, she's perfect."

"He. It's a boy cat. But the original owner called him Cookie, and he knows that name."

"That's fine." I reached into the box and lifted the kitten into my arms. It purred happily and yawned up at me. Bee stroked its fluffy ears and scratched behind them. "He's perfect, Jamie. I could just cry. This is the best gift."

"Good," he said, "because I wanted—"

My phone rang on the table, nearly buzzing off the edge, and I grabbed for it. Bee beat me to it and answered. She listened to the person on the other end, her eyes widening. She covered the phone's receiver and looked over at me.

"It's the alarm company," she hissed. "There's been a break-in at the bakery."

Five

"IT'S PROBABLY NOTHING," I SAID hopefully.

Jamie directed his black Jeep Grand Wagoneer—a change from the Porsche that I figured meant he was ready for a family bigger than just us two—down Clue Street. All the streets in Mystery had ridiculously cute names that suited the town perfectly.

"Probably," Jamie said.

"You two are deluding yourselves." Bee was the voice of my inner landscape, ensconced in the leather seats behind us. "You know it's going to be *something*. It's always *something* with us."

"Bee."

"Remember the time we witnessed a murder?" Bee asked.

"Which time?"

"Exactly my point," Bee said, sounding self-satisfied. "We're magnets for disaster. We're bound to find the bakery in ruins, or on fire, or some madman on the loose, or that the jewelry store has been robbed and the thieves are hiding out in the bakery waiting to pounce."

"Is this the hill you want to die on?" Jamie asked.

Bee wriggled her nose from side-to-side. "Not particularly. For once, I'd like to be wrong."

"What did the alarm company say exactly?" Jamie asked.

"That there was movement inside the bakery," Bee said. "They have those different zones for areas inside and outside, and the doors and windows."

I frowned. "Only movement inside? Well, that could easily be a cat or something."

Bee made a noise in her throat but didn't comment.

We reached Brewer Street—where most of the stores and restaurants were located—and Jamie directed the car into an empty spot in front of the bakery. Clouds had drifted in front of the moon, and the night was pitch black.

The bakery sat in silence, its glass front doors shut tight.

"See?" I swallowed. "It's quiet. There aren't any dark forces at play."

"We don't know that yet," Bee said. "We haven't gone inside."

"We should wait for the alarm company to —" Jamie was interrupted by the slam of the back door.

Bee, always ready to rush head first into danger, was already on her way over to the bakery doors. I got out and followed her, my nerves building with every step. Bee had already fished her set of keys out of her pocket, complete with a cute golden bee keychain, and inserted them into the lock on the front door.

"Maybe Jamie's right," I said, glancing back at my fiancé. He sat in the car behind the wheel, shaking his head at us. He was used to our gung-ho attitude by now, but that didn't mean he liked it.

"It's my experience that men aren't often right, Ruby," Bee said, turning the key in the lock. "And when they are, it's usually twice a day, like a stopped clock."

Jamie's car door slammed. "I heard that."

"Not very progressive of you, Bee," I said.

"I was kidding." Bee rolled her eyes at us. "Some of my favorite people are men." She unlocked the bakery door, and we stepped inside hurriedly. She closed it again, and I disarmed the alarm, the beeps the only sound in the bakery interior.

"What's that smell?" I wrinkled my nose. "It's very..." And then a combination of memories hit me. I had smelled this before, under other unfortunate circumstances. My stomach turned. "Oh no—"

Bee let out a grunt like she'd been hit in the stomach and reached for my hand in the dark. She squeezed it, but my palm was too sweaty and limp to respond.

"What's wrong?" Jamie asked. "What's going on?" He flicked on the lights.

The smell, metallic, had invaded my nostrils, and I squeezed my eyes shut in the sudden influx of light, hoping I wouldn't see *it*. A crime scene.

Bee tensed next to me.

"Again?" I asked in a whisper. "Really?"

"Yes," she said, sounding sturdy as a rock.

Jamie had gone silent.

I opened my eyes, mentally steeling myself for what I'd see. It didn't work. Of course, it didn't work. Seeing a dead body was never easy, especially not one that had been murdered.

Bee released my hand and brought her cellphone out of her pocket, she unlocked it and started taking pictures of the crime scene. She always did that whenever this happened—which it did with surprising frequency.

"Stop," Jamie said. "We have to call 911."

"You call 911, Hanson," Bee replied. "We'll be right here, waiting."

"You can't touch anything."

Bee gave him a look fraught with impatience. This wasn't our first rodeo.

I stared at my fiancé in all his handsomeness, the wrinkles around his eyes a better view than the crime scene. But my gaze drifted over to the body in the center of our precious bakery, as if I had been drawn to look at it against my will.

I sucked in a gasp.

The man had been stabbed in the back with one of Bee's knives. I'd bought her the engraved set as a gift after we'd opened the bakery.

And worse, the victim was familiar.

"It's the ring man." I clapped a hand over my mouth, swallowing hard.

"The ring man?" Jamie shifted as if to walk over to us. We'd been frozen in the same spots since he'd turned on the lights, partly because we didn't want to mess up the crime scene, and partly out of shock. At least for me it was the shock.

"The man who's resizing my ring," I said.

"You're having your ring resized?"

"Yeah," I said. "It kept falling off."

"Why didn't you say anything?" Jamie asked. "That's so weird. I had that ring sized to your—"

"I don't see how that's relevant, Hanson," Bee said, lowering herself to her haunches and getting far too many pictures for my liking.

"Bee and I brought him the ring this afternoon. His name is Cody," I said. "He works at the jewelry store next-door." I chewed on the inside of my cheek. "But how did he get in here? How? If the front door was locked..."

"We should check the door that leads out of the kitchen," Bee said, rising.

"No." Jamie put out a hand. He'd been a detective in a small town not long ago but had retired after several *complications*. He was a stickler for playing by the rules. "Don't move. We've contaminated this crime scene enough. I'm calling 911."

"He's right, Bee," I said. "We should step outside."

Bee gave me a long-suffering look, but followed me out of our bakery and into the night. The wind had an icy nip to it that cut right through my thick, wooly sweater. I shivered and hugged myself, partly because of the cold, but mostly because it had happened again.

An innocent man had been murdered. In our bakery.

I'd hoped that moving to Mystery would signal the end of our investigating habit, but who was I kidding? Bee was right. We were magnets for this kind of stuff. Even without the food truck—which I'd thought was cursed for a while —we were in the middle of another mystery again.

I wasn't sure whether I was frustrated or excited or sickened. It was a heady mixture of emotions.

Bee held me by the arm like I needed steadying. "Are you all right?" she asked.

Jamie peered over at me as he talked on the phone to the 911 operator.

"I'm fine," I said. "I think. I just don't get it."

"Me neither," Bee replied. "How did he get into the locked bakery?"

"Not what I meant," I said. "I was thinking more like... why is there another dead body in our path?"

Bee shrugged. "I don't know. But it's going to be an interesting week."

Six

DETECTIVE WINTERS LED ME INTO THE interrogation room at the Mystery Police Department and sat me in a gray plastic chair in front of a steel desk that reminded me of the counters in the kitchen at the bakery. Except there wouldn't be any sweet treats on offer here. Then again, I'd served Winters this morning—he was the gruff detective who loved donuts. Maybe he'd hidden one around here somewhere?

You're not thinking straight.

That was normal, right? I'd found a dead body in the bakery.

This was a first. We'd never owned a bakery,

only a baking food truck, so technically we'd never found a body in *our* bakery. Just literally everywhere else.

The detective smiled at me, showing me slightly crooked but remarkably white teeth. The impression of a bear with pink cheeks returned.

"Miss Holmes," he said, "thank you for being so eager to talk to me today."

"I'm here as a witness, right?" He hadn't read me any rights, other than witness rights off the back of a small white card.

"Yeah. As we discussed."

"OK." I swallowed.

I had been in situations like this before, but that didn't keep my nerves at bay. Cody was dead. I had barely known the man, but that didn't mean I was anything other than upset about his passing. And in such a visceral way.

Don't think about it. I'd come a long way from wanting to pass out every time I saw blood or found a dead body—a surprisingly frequent occurrence—but that didn't mean I was super comfortable with this.

"I've already taken your statement," Detective Winters said, "but I'd like to go over a few things with you. It's important that you answer my questions in as much detail as possible. If you got a strange feeling about something, or you noticed anything at the scene or related to the victim, I want to know about it."

My shoulders relaxed. It wasn't often we encountered detectives in small towns who were interested in our observations. Refreshing. "I'll help in whatever way I can."

"Fantastic," Detective Winters said, his voice deep and gravelly. "You mentioned that you knew the victim."

"Yeah. He worked at the jewelry store next door to our bakery," I said.

"How well did you know him?"

"Not well," I said. "I met him briefly this morning because I needed to get my engagement ring resized. My fiancé, Jamie? He got the ring designed specifically for me, but it didn't fit right and kept falling off my finger, so I had to get it resized."

"That must have been annoying." Detective Winters tipped his head to one side in understanding.

"It was a bit annoying, yeah," I said. "But it

wasn't a big deal. I went and dropped off the ring this morning before noon."

"And how was Cody when you saw him?"

"OK, I guess. I mean, he seemed a little shifty, if I'm honest. I don't know if that was because his boss was there."

"His boss?" Detective Winters asked.

"Yes," I replied. "Mr. Baron. He's the owner of Baron's Jewelers. He seemed tough on Cody, but not in a mean way. I think. I don't know."

Detective Winters lifted a page on his notepad and checked an item. "So you weren't good friends with Cody?"

"No."

"But you knew his wife intimately," Detective Winters said.

"His wife?" I blinked. "No, I don't believe I do."

"Moira Marks is your wedding planner, isn't she?"

I sucked in a breath. "Yeah, but... Wait, I had no idea she was married to Cody. That's brand new information."

"How long have you been working with Moira for? Or, let me rephrase that, for how long have you had Moira working on your wedding?" Winters asked.

"Oh, a few months now," I said. "She's been handling everything for me. I mean, obviously I still have to make decisions, but she's been great."

"And in all that time, she didn't discuss her husband with you?"

"No," I said. "We kept our conversations professional. About the wedding."

"And you've never encountered Moira out of work with her husband?"

"No, sir," I said, trying to make myself seem open and honest. Funny thing was, I *was* being open and honest, but I felt pressure to prove that now. Which probably had the opposite effect. Sweat gathered on the back of my neck.

The detective fell silent and stared at me for a few moments.

The urge to fill that space nearly overwhelmed me, but what else could I say?

"So, you gave Cody your engagement ring this morning," Detective Winters said, bringing a dossier on the table toward himself. He flipped it open and paged through the documents inside.

"Yeah."

"And then, this evening, your alarm goes off inside your closed bakery," he continued.

"Yeah."

"The bakery that only you and your business partner have keys for."

"Yes." *Oh boy, here we go.*

"You find the victim has been murdered with an engraved knife that comes from your kitchen." Winters was on a roll now. He lifted a picture from the dossier and placed it on the table in front of me, turning it so I could see it without leaning forward. "Is this your engagement ring, Miss Holmes?"

And so it was. A picture of my engagement ring—the platinum band, the gorgeous cluster of diamonds. Except it was tinged... red? "Yeah, that's my ring. Where did you—?"

"Cody Marks was found clutching your engagement ring in his right hand," he said. "In your locked bakery. Stabbed with your friend's knife."

My face flushed red. I opened my mouth to say something, but no words came out.

"Your wedding planner was married to the victim. You saw the victim on the morning of the day of his death."

Still couldn't form a word.

"Would you say those statements are correct?"

I nodded.

"Would you *say* they're correct, Miss Holmes?" Detective Winters repeated.

"Yes, they're correct."

He stared at me without shifting an inch.

"I thought I was here as a witness," I said.

"You are."

"I'm willing to cooperate with you fully, but if you're accusing me or my friend of murder, you're just plain wrong. We were at our house with my fiancé all evening. And we received the call from the alarm company while at my house. Also, why would I stab a man and then set off an alarm in my own locked bakery." The heat remained in my face, but this time it was due to irritation rather than fear.

Did this detective really think he was going

to crack the case and me? He had another think coming.

"I'm merely asking questions, Miss Holmes?"

"Am I free to go?" I countered, channeling Bee's energy for once. I wasn't going to start off my time in Mystery, Maine, as a pushover. If this was going to be our town then I had to set the tone. And that tone would be extricating myself from this mess with as much grace as I could muster.

Detective Winters stalled.

"Am I free to go?" I repeated. "Or do I need to get a lawyer?"

"Currently," Detective Winters said, "you're free to go."

"Thank you." I rose from my seat. Helping the police was one thing, but I wasn't going to hang around while he tried to wrangle a confession out of me. Detective Winters escorted me from the interrogation room.

"I'll be in touch," he said. "Don't leave town."

Seven

The following morning...

"I can't believe it." Leslie sat in my favorite living room chair—a comfy leather lounger that was perfect for reading—a mug of hot chocolate tucked between her palms. She stared first at me then at Bee, wide-eyed.

Bee had positioned herself on the sofa nearest the fireplace, a fire crackling merrily behind the grate, and darted a feathery toy across her lap, smiling in delight when Cookie the kitten chased it.

"We're going to have to stay closed for a while," I said. "Until the police release the scene, and we're allowed to go in and clean and re-order everything."

"Clean." Leslie gulped. "But they're not gonna make us clean the... you know. The—"

"Blood?" Bee asked. "No, they usually have teams that do that. Crime scene cleanup. But we'll naturally do a full cleaning of our own. You know, we could pivot and use this to our advantage." Bee's tone was businesslike but stiff. The bakery was her dream, and I doubted she liked the idea of closing up for any length of time.

"Our advantage?" I asked. "How?"

"A relaunch. We'll design a specific treat and host a relaunch party. Heavens, it's close to Halloween, we could use the murder as a selling point."

"Bee!"

"What?" She chased the feather toy across the back of the sofa, and Cookie went wild across the top of it, clawing and scratching. I foresaw a lot of marked up furniture in my future.

"That's crass, even for you. Cody died yesterday."

"I know, I know," Bee said without looking up. "It's just frustrating. Everything was falling into place."

I privately agreed.

"I can't believe he's dead," Leslie whispered. "Cody was a nice guy. For the most part."

"The most part?" Bee's head snapped up. She couldn't resist a lead.

Leslie jerked a little under her gaze, sploshing hot chocolate onto her lap. I hurried through to the kitchen and returned with a napkin.

"—argued with her." Leslie accepted the napkin and dabbed her lap. "Thanks, Ruby."

"Who are we talking about?" I asked.

"Apparently Cody and his wife, your wedding planner, had been having marital issues," Bee said instantly.

I pressed my lips together and released them slowly. "That doesn't mean anything, though. I highly doubt Moira would have done this."

"We can't highly doubt anything without

the facts, Ruby," Bee said. "You know that."

"I do. But I don't want to know that. And before you ask, Bee, I don't think it's a good idea."

Cookie scratched the back of the sofa impatiently. Bee had stopped fiddling around with the feather. "Why not?" Bee asked. "It's always a good idea with us. And you did mention the detective was a little rough around the edges with you."

"You didn't get the same impression?" I asked.

Two pink spots appeared in Bee's cheeks. "No. He was thorough and professional, but that doesn't mean I trust his methods."

Leslie's head whipped back and forth as she watched us serve and volley.

"Bee. This is a new town. We said we wouldn't get involved in this type of thing anymore." I was as curious as she was, but to step on the cops' toes again? I wasn't sure I was up for it. Not with Jamie searching for a position in town, and with everything else we had going on. Besides, I wasn't even sure I could trust myself to—

"I'm lost," Leslie said, "what are you talking

about?"

I bit down on the inside of my cheek. Bee sighed.

"It's complicated to explain," Bee said. "I used to be a cop. Ruby was an investigative journalist. We like to check things out, especially murders. Huh. I guess it's not that complicated to explain."

"You've done something like that before?" Leslie asked.

"Sure," Bee said.

"But that doesn't mean we're going to do it again."

Bee barely contained an eye roll and turned to Leslie. "What else can you tell us about Cody," she said. "What about his working relationship with Mr. Baron."

"Mr. Baron? He's a rig," Leslie said. "And he's difficult to work for, from what I've heard. But I didn't hear him and Cody going at it. He was barely around for that to happen."

"Who?" I asked, in spite of myself. "Mr. Baron?"

"Ayuh." Leslie took another sip of hot chocolate. "My mother used to work for him back years ago, before she adopted me, and she said that he was terminally bored with life."

"Oh?" Bee leaned forward.

"Always moving from one place to another. Before he owned the jewelry store, he had a florist shop, and before that a restaurant. He's got plenty of money to go around, or he did before this year." Leslie paused. "I heard that he's having some money troubles now."

"Where did you hear that?" Bee asked.

"Just around. People talk in this town." Leslie shrugged her skinny shoulders and took another mouthful of hot chocolate.

Bee's eyes had narrowed nearly to slits. "So, we've got a jewelry store next door that's running out of money, a victim clutching a ring, and marital problems."

"You're forgetting the fact that we have no idea how Cody even got into the bakery. Or how the murderer did for that matter. None of this makes much sense," I said.

"Murders never make sense," Bee replied, lifting the feather and dancing it around for Cookie again. The kitten gave a tempestuous purring meow before taking up the chase again.

"They're called a senseless crime for a reason. That's why it's so fun to solve them."

"And because you're bringing a murderer to justice," I said.

"That too." Bee gave me a sly smile, like she'd hooked me into admitting that I wanted to investigate.

Leslie watched the exchange curiously, and I didn't blame her. We'd worked with her for a few months, but she had no information about our pasts, other than that we'd decided to settle in Maine after traveling through several states on our baking food truck. And now our past professions.

My stomach panged at the memory of our truck, and the freedom that had come from traveling through small towns and serving our treats. I missed it, but I wouldn't give this life up for that one.

Or would you?

"So," Leslie said, "what are you going to do?"

I remained silent.

Bee's smile broadened. "Well, we have to face facts," she said, as Cookie darted across her lap again. "Detective Winters is interested in us as suspects. Why wouldn't he be? We own the bakery and the murder weapon, and the set of keys that unlocks the door behind which the body was found."

"He won't find our fingerprints on the weapon," I said.

"No," Bee replied. "But that doesn't matter. He's going to keep pulling on that string. And who knows how long it will take them to process a crime scene in this town—"

"We haven't had a murder here in years," Leslie said. "There's been the usual stuff, but not a murder in a while. The last time was when Uncle Greg got pushed off his boat out in the bay. They thought it was an accident for a while before they figured out what happened."

I didn't particularly like where this conversation was going, even if I did have a certain excitement brewing in my gut about the prospect of investigating a murder. I opened my mouth to say as much, but my phone buzzed on the coffee table before I could.

I leaned forward. Moira's name flashed on the screen. "I'd better take this."

Eight

"Moira," I said, as pleasantly as I could. "How are you holding up?"

A lengthy sigh was the response. This was not unlike Moira. She wasn't exactly the peppiest woman around. Her responses to my questions varied from sighs to the occasional unhappy moan. The only time I'd seen her happy was when she was in florist shops picking out flowers or helping someone set up their online wedding registry.

"Things are difficult," Moira said, her voice a slow drawl. "My husband has been murdered."

"I'm so sorry for your loss, Moira."

A pause. Another sigh. An unhappy moan. "Me too," she said.

Strangely, she didn't sound any more upset than she usually did when we talked. *You're reading into it too much. She's distraught. Or dealing with her grief in her own way.* "If there's anything I can do to help you, anything at all, please just let me know."

"There's one thing you can do," Moira said.

"What is it?" I asked.

"Find another wedding planner."

My stomach dropped like a rock. "Oh."

"Sorry, Ruby," she said. "But my husband is gone, and he was found dead in your bakery. The cops told me as much. I—I've got stuff to deal with."

"Moira, I—"

"I can't do it, OK?" A sob came down the line.

"I understand," I said. "I completely understand. You let me know if you need anything else, OK? Bee and I would be happy to help you with—"

"You've done enough." She hung up.

The dull click had been so final, but I pulled

the phone away from my ear to check that she'd disconnected. For all her moaning and complaints—prior to her husband dying, of course—Moira was a fantastic wedding planner. She'd helped me out loads, and it was going to be tough to progress without her, especially with the bakery going through, well, what it was going through right now.

Nerves burst to life in my belly, followed by an aching pain.

"Ruby?" Bee stood in the doorway to the living room. "Are you OK?"

"Moira just pulled out of the wedding," I said. "She's upset about her husband, but... it was more than that. I think she believes that I had something to do with what happened to him."

Bee folded her arms, frowning. "That or she's hiding something and doesn't want anyone to find out what it is."

Leslie peeked around the corner. "What's going on?"

"My wedding planner pulled out of my wedding," I said. "I'm going to have to find another planner."

"But it's only a couple of months to go, isn't it?" Leslie asked.

I nodded.

"Hmm." Bee scratched her chin.

"What is it, Bee?" I asked.

"I think we should pay Moira a visit," she said. "Offer our condolences. Maybe take a couple of donuts with us."

Leslie swallowed audibly. "Count me out. Moira's not my type of people, if you know what I mean. And by that I mean, she's kind of mean."

Mean. She'd always been kind to me, but maybe that was because I'd been her client. Was I really going to go with Bee's plan to talk to her? "Offering our condolences" had long since become a euphemism for talking to the family of the deceased about the victim.

Bee raised a silver eyebrow at me, mischief in her gaze.

"Let's do it," I said.

TWO HOURS LATER, AFTER WE'D BAKED
donuts in the kitchen and fed our sweetheart,
Cookie, we headed out toward Moira's house.
I'd been to her small cottage near the ocean once
before, and it was when she'd asked me to come
over and look at her themed book of ideas for
the wedding. Cody certainly hadn't been there at
the time, and there hadn't been wedding pictures on the walls.

Why wouldn't she put up wedding pictures?
Moira was a wedding planner, so surely her own
wedding had been fabulous?

Mystery, Maine, was situated along a small
bay, with most of the real estate facing toward
the ocean. There were a few fishermen on the
docks as we drove by, as well as lobster boats that
had come in from their early morning and
parked along the many jetties. Oceanside Lane
ran all along the coast and the offshoots housed a
lot of prime real estate—many of which were the
vacation homes of "flatlanders."

"It's a nice day," I said, peering up at the
cloudless sky.

"For fall, you mean." Bee couldn't stand the

cold and had already put on a pink puffy coat that whispered when she moved her arms.

I parked my car—a navy blue Chevrolet Cruze—outside Moira's cottage then got out. The smell of salty air and the distant rush of ocean waves set me at ease. I loved the ocean, but I preferred our double story tucked away between the trees and removed from most of the town.

"The curtains are drawn," Bee said, joining me with a box clasped in both hands.

And indeed, both the front windows of the cottage which sat either side of the door, like two eyes, were dark, curtains closed and lights off.

"Maybe she's not home," I said.

Bee didn't give up that easily. She marched up the garden path and onto the cute wooden front porch, which had a fine dusting of white sand on it as if the occupants had just gotten back from the beach.

I tucked my coat close to my body and followed her.

Bee's insistent knocking would have woken the dead. *Poor choice of words.*

"Hello?" Bee called. "Moira. You in there?"

Quiet, and then the gentle clack of kitten heels. I imagined Moira in her professional pumps approaching the door, the corners of her mouth turned down as they always were—a permanent look of disapproval. Or sadness.

"Who's that?" Moira asked.

"Bee," my friend said. "From Bee's Bakery. And Ruby."

"You shouldn't have come here." The hiss came through the bleached wood door.

"We came to give you our condolences," Bee said, sounding completely unsympathetic.

"And to offer you a few donuts," I put in, in a milder tone. "This must be a very difficult time for you, Moira. We're so sorry for your loss."

A few moments passed, and then the door opened. Moira wore her usual outfit—black pumps, pantsuit, her hair up in a bun, but her frown was more pronounced than usual.

"Here you go," Bee said, depositing the box into her hands. "They're filled with raspberry coulis, oven-baked so they're light and crispy, and coated in fine sugar."

Moira licked her lips. "Thank you."

"Are you OK, Moira?" I asked. "Silly question, I know, but I wanted to check."

Moira tapped her neatly clipped nails on the top of the box of donuts. "I'm good as I can be. I just—" She peered up and down the street. "Don't want to talk to anybody. The police have already come by and warned me not to say anything."

"Say anything?" Bee asked. "About what?"

"I shouldn't have said that," Moira replied. "I just—they seem to think that maybe you two will interfere in what happened to Cody. In the m-m—"

"His unfortunate passing," I said, before Bee blurted out the word "murder."

"They said they think we'll get involved? Or that we *are* involved?" Bee asked.

"I don't know the difference. I don't want to get in trouble." She made to close the door. Bee slapped a palm against it, and Moira let out an unhappy sigh.

"Oh no," she whispered. "Here we go. Of course, this is happening to me. This kind of thing always happens to me. Why? I don't deserve this do I? I feel like I've paid my dues, and I—"

Bee clicked her tongue. "Moira," she said, "what can you tell us about your husband?"

"What do you mean?"

"Has he been acting different lately? Any red flags you noticed?"

"I—" Moira cut off.

"Bee's asking because this happened in *our* bakery," I said, to try to dissolve some of the tension. "Try" being the operative word. "And we want to make sure that the police have all the correct information."

"The more you talk, the more you sound like you're threatening her," Bee said.

"Huh?" I blinked. "I do?"

"Sure," Bee laughed. "Next you're going to ask for a favor or something."

"I didn't mean it like that," I said.

"I know that, but she doesn't. Look at her. She's shaking in her perfectly sensible pumps."

Moira's lower lip trembled. "He was meeting with people," she said. "He was—"

"Who?" Bee and I asked, turning our gazes in her direction.

Moira paled. "I don't know, but he'd go down to the Claw Pot and catch a buzz on a few nights a week. He never did that before."

"Did he do that last night?" I asked.

"I don't know," she said. "I was asleep. But now, I've gotta go. Got to put these on ice." She lifted the donuts. "I mean, I've got to put them in the cellar, I mean the—" And then she shut the door in our faces.

Bee and I shared a look fraught with curiosity. The spouse had no alibi. And she was nervous. So nervous she'd given us information willingly.

What was she hiding?

Nine

Later that afternoon...

THE CLAW POT HAD AN OCEAN VIEW, hardwood floors, and seating that was rustic and family style. Thankfully, there were a few private booths along the walls, overlooking the tumultuous ocean and the gray-blue sky.

Bee and I sat across from each other, eyeing the menu—a laminated piece of paper with red lobsters printed along the borders—and occasionally the other diners. A family of five had positioned themselves at a central table and had already put on plastic bibs over their "I heart Maine" sweatshirts.

Even at this time of year, or maybe, especially at this time of year, tourists trickled in from far and wide.

I rested my chin on my fist and peered out of the sea-sprayed windows at the docks below. "Jamie should be here," I sighed.

"He's been keeping himself busy lately."

I nodded. "It's the job hunt. I wish he'd find something already. But then, I'm not sure I want him to."

"The most likely job will be in the police department," Bee said. "That will be difficult for us. And for him."

She was, of course, referring to our penchant for sticking our noses where they didn't belong. But old habits died hard. Or not at all in this case. A good thing, since there'd been more than enough death in Mystery of late.

"What do you think?" I asked.

Bee looked up from her menu. "Two things," she said, raising the corresponding number of fingers. "That I'm going to try the soft shell crab, and that we're going to have to find a server who was working on the night of Cody's murder. Hopefully, one of them will be able to give us an identification for the guy he was meeting."

"Or the woman," I said. "We don't know *who* he was meeting yet."

"True." Bee shifted her menu aside.

I tucked my hands into my lap and continued scanning the activity on the docks below. There was something about that scurry of activity that comforted my soul. Or maybe it was that the first murder we'd ever investigated had been the death of a fisherman in Maine. Things had come full circle, almost.

"Afternoon." Our server, roundish with a friendly albeit weary expression, stood next to our table. "Name's Kristen. What can I get for you ladies this fine afternoon?"

"Hi Kristen," I said. "I'd like a chocolate milkshake and a lobster roll, please."

"Same milkshake and the soft shell crab."

"Get that for you right away," she said, turning to go. She was the type of server who didn't need a pen or a notepad, and the heels of her sneakers were worn through.

"Wait a second," Bee said. "We've got a question for you."

Kristen forced a smile. A long-suffering one. Doubtless, she thought we were "flatlanders" who had questions about tourist attractions. Or maybe it had been a long morning.

A burst of raucous laughter came from the center table, and a man raised a greasy hand to summon help then let out a yipping whistle when it wasn't forthcoming. Oh yeah, it had definitely been a long day for Kristen.

She turned and glared at him. "Just one darn second," she yelled back.

He lowered his greasy paw before he lost it.

"What do you need to know?" she asked.

Bee and I both shifted closer to her, and she watched our movements through narrowed eyes.

"You heard about the death of Cody Marks, I assume?" Bee asked.

Kristen's eyes narrowed even further, so that they were barely perceptible slivers. "What 'bout it?"

"Did you notice Cody meeting with anyone

at this restaurant? On Tuesday night?"

Kristen didn't say anything for a moment.

"We're not cops," I said. "We're just curious. Cody died in our bakery."

"Oh, so you're the flatlanders who moved out to the old haunted house," she said.

"Haunted?" I blinked.

Bee waved away the comment. "Sure," she said. "Now, did you see Cody meeting with anyone?"

"Don't know his name, but he talked my ear darn near off when I waited on their table," she said. "He grew up in The County. Acted like a dubbah, but according to Cody, he's not."

"A dubbah?" I was still getting used to the colloquialisms in Maine.

"Yeah." She tapped the side of her head. "Not all there? Not switched on? Two branches short of a tree? But he's smart. Has to be if he's doing that stuff with computers." She smacked her lips. "That's what Cody said, anyway. That he was some IT guy helping with stuff at the jewelry store. But I figured that the Baron would be talking to him about stuff like that. Cody wasn't a manager or anything."

"So, this guy that was with Cody. The stupid-smart guy," Bee said, "what did he look like? And was he here with Cody often?"

"A few times over the last month," Kristen said. "But I never bothered asking what his name was. Didn't think he'd be hanging around for long. He kept mentioning how he was passing through."

"And his looks?" Bee prompted, never one to lose track of the topic.

"Oh, taller than a tree and kinda cunnin'." Kristens cheeks reddened. "Dark hair, blue eyes, nice full lips, with a beard."

"What time were they here?" We hadn't yet established a timeline for the murder.

"Oh, around about 07:30 p.m., I think and they—"

The greasy-handed guy at the center table whistled again. Kristen rolled her eyes and excused herself, leaving Bee and me to consider our new lead.

A handsome guy who was good with computers. Possibly from out of town. Or gone by now for that matter.

We had to find him.

Ten

THE FOLLOWING MORNING, WE STILL
hadn't heard anything from the police about the
crime scene being released which meant we
didn't have a bakery to run. And life was only
going to get more frustrating. Last night, after
Bee and I had arrived back from the Claw Pot,
our bellies stuffed with good food and our brains
brimming with questions, we'd met none other
than Detective Winters on the front porch.

He'd been bent over, studying the railing.

"Detective Winters?" Bee said. "What are
you—?"

He snapped upright. "Ladies. I was hoping to catch up with you."

"About what?"

"I got a call from the Marks widow," he said. "Apparently you were over there plying her with donuts and asking questions about the victim. Is that true?"

I swallowed my words, hoping Bee would handle it. She pressed a hand to her stomach. "No idea what you're talking about, Detective."

Winters grunted then strolled down the path to meet us. "Just watch what you say and who you say it too, all right?" The growl was thick and deep. His cologne drifted on the air—a not unpleasant leathery scent.

Bee hadn't said a word in response—most unlike her.

With that, he'd left us standing out in the cold air. And Jamie had come home moments later to find us standing there.

"Ruby?" Bee peeped in through the open archway that led from the living room to the sunlit kitchen. "Are you—?"

"Fine, sorry. I'm coming!" I'd prepared a tray

of hot chocolate and cookies. This time, we were plying Leslie with food rather than my wedding planner. She would be less likely to run to Detective Winters with the news that we were asking questions.

I walked through the dining area and into the living room where Leslie had chosen my favorite lazy armchair. She thanked me for the hot chocolate and smiled at Cookie, who was draped over another armchair in front of the window, sunning his furry belly.

"I wonder," I said, "why the widow outed us to Detective Winters."

Bee cleared her throat and didn't answer.

"Bee?"

"Hmm?"

"Why do you think Moira did that?" I asked. "It wasn't like we pressured her too much. But she was acting kind of shifty." She didn't have an alibi, and then there was the fact that she'd looked ready to jump out of her skin every time we asked a question.

"Moira did what now?" Leslie asked.

I explained it to her briefly, frowning at Bee.

My friend was not acting her usual self, and she avoided my gaze by fixating on Cookie.

"I bet it's because she had something to do with Cody's murder," Leslie said instantly.

"You think so?" Finally, Bee looked up.

"Rumor has it that she's the one who's going to inherit all of Cody's money," Leslie said. "Not that he had much, but she's his wife and she was in his will. And everyone was saying she'd been having an affair."

"You know that for sure?" I asked.

"Just a rumor," Leslie replied. "But where there's smoke there's a fire, right?"

Bee wrinkled up her nose. "We wanted to ask you about something specific."

"What is it?" Leslie took a sip of her hot chocolate and savored it. "Is it to do with Cody's murder? I'm starting to get into this. The whole 'investigating' thing is kinda fun."

If only you knew. Solving mysteries was exhausting, fun, and scary wrapped up in one murder-shaped bundle.

Bee filled Leslie in on what we'd discovered at the Claw Pot. "So, what do you think? Do you recognize that description?"

"Cunnin'?" Leslie fingered her chin. "Cunnin'? And with a dark beard and blue eyes. Dark hair and tall like a house. Did she say whether he was strong or not? Big muscles? Nah, it doesn't matter. There are two guys in town who match that description, and one of them has left to go on a cruise."

"Who are they?" Bee asked, lifting a cookie from the saucer on the tray. She snapped it in half before taking a bite.

"Tom Riezl," Leslie said, "who is a mechanic and has run off with his mistress on a cruise. So, he couldn't have been here on Tuesday night."

"And who was the other one, Leslie?" I stood near the fireplace, warming myself.

"He's new to town," Leslie said. "Hasn't been here long, but I heard he wants to open his own IT store or something to do with computers."

"That's got to be the guy." Bee clicked her fingers.

"He came through once before but left again. I didn't think he'd be back but he came through again at the beginning of fall."

"You're killing us here," Bee said. "What's his name?"

"Oh, sorry," Leslie giggled, "I was thinking out loud. His name is Redford Smalls. He's from The County, I think, but he's pretty mysterious. Nobody knows much about him other than the whole IT thing. You said he was hanging out with Cody?"

"Right before he died," Bee said.

"Huh. I think he's been staying at the guesthouse up the road apiece," Leslie said. "So if you want to talk to him, I guess he's close by at least."

"Are you talking about the Carriage House?" I asked.

"That's the one," Leslie replied. "Grant owns the place. Have you met him yet?"

"I think so," I said. "He came by on the first night we moved in. Remember him, Bee?"

"Hmm." My best friend tapped her chin. "Hmm."

She was too lost in thought to respond. Either way, we had the lead we needed. The name of the guy who had been meeting with the victim. If we could establish a timeline of what had happened that night, we could track down the killer.

We'd start with this Redford Smalls guy and work our way forward until the proposed time of the murder, which had to have been some time between 06:00 p.m., when we'd set the alarm and locked up the bakery, and after 08:00 p.m., when we'd received the call from the alarm company.

That was a window of about two and a half hours when something could have happened. But Kristen had told us that Cody and this Redford guy had been at the Claw Pot at 07:30 p.m.. That left approximately one hour since he'd last been seen alive.

And it seemed like Redford Smalls was the person who'd last been seen with Cody.

I gnawed on the inside of my cheek and walked over to the windows, pausing to scratch the underside of Cookie's soft furry chin.

"What do you think, Bee?" I asked. "Should we pay Mr. Smalls a visit?"

"It's not even a question," she replied. "Let's finish our cookies and go."

"What if we run into the detective on the

way there." I turned my head to gauge her reaction. She didn't see me watching, but she did lower her head and fiddle with her pleated wool skirt.

"I'm sure we won't," she said, a tiny smile on her lips.

Eleven

THE CARRIAGE HOUSE WAS HIDDEN between the trees down a dirt road, much like our "fixer-upper", but its shiplap walls were painted a steely gray, and the doors and windows accented with white. It had three floors, and could have easily seemed intimidating, but the rustle of wind and falling leaves and the warm flickering light from the front windows extended an invitation.

I parked my car in the designated gravel parking area out front. "We really need to decorate for Halloween," I said absently.

"What on earth made you think of that?" Bee asked.

Leslie had turned down our offer to come along to the Carriage House, opting instead to go visit her adoptive mother who lived on the other side of town.

"Just look at this place. Don't you think it looks like a place a witch would set up her home? It's spooky but sort of intriguing. Very Halloweeny."

"Halloweeny," Bee laughed.

"What? It is."

"Next you'll start believing the rumors about your house being haunted."

I gave a fake shudder, and Bee sent me a grin. We got out of the car and made our way up to the front of the building. The wooden porch creaked underfoot, and the soft sound of smooth jazz echoed from within the building.

Bee knocked once on the double doors before opening one of them and entering.

Grant, the owner of the Carriage House, looked up from the reception desk and smiled at us broadly. "Hello ladies," he said. "Welcome to the Carriage House. What can I do you for?"

"Morning, Grant," I said. "It's nice to see you again. Do you remember us?"

"Of course. My neighbors from up the road apiece."

Bee drew closer to the reception desk. The stereo behind it was the source of the music, and a quick glance through the door—open a crack to our left—showed a welcoming fire crackling in a grate beyond.

"You have a guest here by the name of Redford Smalls," Bee said. "Is he around? We want to talk to him about something serious."

"Serious?"

"Yeah."

Grant puffed out his cheeks and exhaled. "Hard tellin', not knowin'. Best guess is he's in his room or out doing whatever it is he does."

So he wasn't around. That put paid to our plans.

If only he—

The front door of the Carriage House opened, and a tall guy with a thick, well-combed beard entered the establishment.

"There he is," Grant said, with more excitement than was strictly necessary. He jumped up and pointed a chubby finger at the man. "That's Mr. Smalls, right there. Hey, Mr. Smalls, these ladies wanted to talk to you about—"

But Redford Smalls didn't give him a chance to finish his sentence. He turned tail and darted out of the front doors.

"Hey!" Bee yelled. "Get back here!" She took off after him.

I squeezed my eyes shut for a moment then followed her, albeit at a slower pace. Redford had much longer legs than me, and I doubted I'd keep up even with sustained effort.

Bee had already made it out into the yard and had chased around the side of the building. Apparently, Redford had opted not to leave the grounds but to circle them—and odd choice. Didn't he have a car? I reached the corner of the Carriage House and searched for signs of the pursuit.

Redford had already reached the corner and Bee was lagging behind him, yelling out his name and trying her best to catch up.

This called for innovation rather than strength.

I hurried to the other corner of the Carriage

House and pressed my back against the wall, waiting, my heart beating a frantic pulse in my ears.

This is silly. You shouldn't even be involved in—

The huff and puff of Redford running down the side of the building started up and grew louder. I had to time this exactly right if I wanted it to work.

Closer. Closer still. He was about to—

There!

Redford turned the corner, and I stuck out my leg. He tripped forward in fantastic fashion, his arms pinwheeling, and fell flat on his face on the grass with a crunch. He groaned and lay still.

I sat down on his back, unceremoniously, my hands pressed down on his shoulders and my feet firmly planted on either side of him.

Bee darted around the corner and skidded to a halt, kicking up a clod of dirt and grass. "Ruby? How did you—?"

"Work smarter, not harder," I replied.

Bee laughed in delight then came over and crouched down in front of Redford. The man was, true to his name, red in the face. "Let go of me," he grunted, and started pushing up.

I clung to him like he was a bucking bronco. "Hey! Easy there."

Bee tapped him once on the head. "Stop moving," she said, "or I'll be forced to pepper spray you." An empty threat since she'd left her purse in the car and the pepper spray was inside it. "Stop!"

"What do you want?" Redford asked. "Unhand me."

"We want to talk," I said. "About Cody Marks."

The man stiffened, and I used the lack of movement to adjust my position on his back and press my weight down further. Hopefully, those extra donuts would pay off.

"I don't know a Cody Marks," he said.

"Liar," Bee replied. "We know you were at the Claw Pot with him hours before his death. And why else would you have run from us unless you knew why we wanted to talk to you?"

"You cops?"

Bee didn't answer him.

I didn't want to either. I wasn't sure whether

it would be better to lie or tell the truth. I normally defaulted to truth, but we were dealing with a potential murderer here.

My phone buzzed in my pocket, and I scrambled it out of my jeans. Jamie's name flashed on the screen.

"Hey, honey," I said. "I'm kind of in the middle of—"

"I got the job!" Jamie cried. "I got it."

"That's incredible!" I replied. "I'm in the middle—"

"I'm going to be a police officer again," he said. "Can you believe it? I'm finally going to be back at work. I never thought this would happen after Muffin, but I—Ruby, I couldn't have done this without you."

"That's not true. You're a great police officer," I replied.

Underneath me, our "perp" stiffened again. Then he started rising. I bit back a yelp as he stood up and deposited me on the ground with a thump.

"We're going out for lunch," Jamie said. "Where are you two? We've got to celebrate."

"Uh... we're just on our way home."

"Good. I'll see you in ten!"

"Love you," I replied, but Jamie had already hung up in his excitement.

Redford glared down at me. "Either you're cops," he said, "and you don't have a right to detain me. Or you're not, and I should be the one calling the cops."

I swallowed. Redford had a mean look about him. A disregard for consequences that sparkled in his deep blue eyes.

"We are..." I glanced up at Bee for her help.

"Leaving," she said. "We're leaving." And then she extended a hand toward me and helped me from the dirt. With our dignity smarting, we strode back to my car. I sensed Redford glaring at our backs but didn't dare see if I was right.

This had been a fruitless endeavor. And now Jamie was going to be a police officer again, things were about to go from complicated and confusing to... Well, it wasn't going to be good, that was for sure.

Twelve

Later that afternoon...

JAMIE HAD TREATED US TO A FANTASTIC
lunch at a farm-to-table restaurant called "Grass-
fed" which specialized in steaks. I'd enjoyed a
hanger steak, while Bee had gone for a pork loin,
and Jamie had barely touched his half-chicken
out of sheer excitement. He was so happy, I
couldn't help being swept up in his joy.

I didn't want to believe that this would affect
our relationship, but I was dubious. Jamie had

to know that we liked to get involved in things. Curiosity had never killed us, but satisfaction had been a constant in our lives ever since we'd decided that we'd leave no stone unturned.

This is bad. You should stop investigating what happened to Cody, right away.

But my desire to prove our innocence and open the bakery again was strong.

Besides, it wasn't like Jamie was going to be a detective. Just a cop. There was a difference.

After our lunch, he dropped us off in Brewer Street. Bee and I wanted to check out a local antique store—or so we'd told him. Really, we wanted to talk to Mr. Baron. Cody's boss.

"I'm sure it won't be as bad as you think," Bee said, as we watched Jamie's SUV drive off. He gave us a jaunty wave out of the window before taking the corner.

"What won't be as bad as I think?"

"Him being a police officer," Bee said. "Remember, when he was working that case in Muffin, he was nice. The campgrounds case."

"I remember," I replied. "But I don't want to mess anything up for him. He's been so supportive. And the other night, he mentioned wanting to run for office."

"To be the president? Of the country?"

"No! Oh, heck no," I said. "At least I hope not. That sounds like a nightmare. I think he wants to be the mayor."

"The mayor of Mystery." Bee liked the idea, apparently. "He would be good at that. And it might give us a certain degree of protection when we're doing all the things we shouldn't."

"That's not what I want. I don't want his endeavors to be tainted by ours."

Bee squeezed my shoulder affectionately but didn't give me a rebuttal. She knew I was right. We were troublemakers, always skirting the law. Doubt tumbled through my belly, but I followed Bee down the road toward Baron's Jewelers, past the closed bakery with its police seal tacked over the keyhole and the side of the door.

"I wonder when they'll be finished," I said. "We could ask Detective Winters about it."

"No!" Bee's answer whipped out of her mouth.

"What is it with you and that detective?" I

asked. "Every time we run into him you clam up."

"I do *not,*" she hissed.

Bee had a crush on him. I was sure of it. I didn't push the issue, though, and instead pressed my finger to the button outside of the jewelry store.

The buzz and clack that followed sent a shiver down my spine. The last time we'd been here, it was to have my ring resized—when Cody had been alive and well.

Why did he have my ring in his hand? And how did he get into the bakery? Both parts of this mystery that I wasn't sure we'd ever solve. The best we could do was follow the clues we had and talk to the people closest to Cody.

So far, Redford Smalls and my wedding planner, Moira, were equally suspicious.

Mr. Baron stood behind the counter in his store, long dark hair tied into a tiny bobble of a bun at the back of his head. He gave us a gaunt and intense stare as we entered.

"Ah," he said, "your ring."

"Good afternoon, Mr. Baron," I replied. "I—"

"I'm afraid I can't give you your ring," he said, bending over the counter and examining a fine watch encrusted with jewels. "You see, it's in the police's hands now."

"I'm not here for the ring," I replied.

He continued examining the watch, and the sleeve of his fine cotton shirt shifted, showing a dark bruise along the back of his wrist.

"Oh," I said. "Are you OK?"

"OK? I've been better," he replied. "I just lost the best employee I've ever had."

"No," I said. "Your wrist."

Mr. Baron drew back his sleeve, shaking his head at the bruise, dismissively. "This silly old thing? I slammed it in the gate the other morning on my way into the store. I've been understandably distracted and upset over the past while. Cody... Cody was a good friend of mine, and now he's gone, I'm not sure how I'm going to keep this store open."

So the rumors about his financial difficulties were true? But how did that factor in to the murder? Even if he'd been struggling, that didn't give him a motive for murdering Cody. It wasn't like he'd inherit any of his money. And if he couldn't afford to keep him as an employee, he could have fired him.

"How are you holding up?" I asked, trying to find a segue that made sense. "How's business?"

"Poor on both accounts," Mr. Baron said. "What did you want to talk to me about?"

"Cody," Bee said, stepping forward from her spot as an observer of the conversation. "We wanted to find out more about him. And if there was anyone suspicious hanging around the jewelry store or Cody himself in the past while."

Mr. Baron finally stopped obsessing over the watch. "Why would you want to know that?"

"Because he died in our bakery," Bee said simply. "And the police think we had something to do with it even though we have an alibi."

Mr. Baron eyed us, and I got the impression of a vampire, risen from his daily slumber to search for new victims. "That's honest of you."

"I'm an honest person," Bee said.

"A regrettable trait."

Bee jerked her head back and opened her mouth to say something, but Mr. Baron waved a long-fingered hand.

"Cody was like a son to me, since my own is so uninterested in anything to do with my life or business. And he was a friend too. A good friend. I didn't hurt him, and I didn't notice anything different about him in the time leading up to his death. I told Detective Winters the same." Marcus Baron paused, drawing himself to his full height, and gave each of us an imperious stare. "Not that I owe you any explanations."

A bell tinkled in the store, and Mr. Baron reached under the counter and pressed a button out of sight. The gate clanged behind us, and a petite woman with wan cheeks, wearing all beige entered the store, holding a tiny dog in her arms.

"Marcus," she breathed.

"Hello, Julia my darling. I'm just with some customers. We'll go to dinner in a moment."

"That's fine." She walked off to one side and waited, still as a rock, as if she could disappear into the scenery in the store. Her eyes darted from left-to-right, constantly, and whenever she looked over at her husband, she would jolt a little and look away again.

Strange. Very strange.

"It's lovely to meet you," I said to her.

She gave me a tiny nod of greeting. She wasn't dressed up like Marcus was, but she was pretty, if a bit plain and tired.

"Is there anything else?" Mr. Baron asked. "I do have *things* to attend to."

"Thank you for your time, Mr. Baron." I took Bee by the arm and we left the jewelry store with more questions than answers.

Thirteen

The following morning, bright and early...

BEE TAPPED HER FINGERS ON THE WHEEL of my car, frowning up at the Carriage House, yawning occasionally, even though she'd already inhaled two custard-filled donuts this morning. "I don't see—" A yawn broke the sentence.

"Don't see?" I had my Notes app open on my phone and was in the process of typing out our suspect and clues list. It was something we'd gotten into the habit of doing on the food truck.

"I don't see—" Another yawn.

"You're going to have to finish one of these sentences."

Bee snorted. "I don't see why we have to come out here at the crack of dawn when we're not even sure if he's in the Carriage House in the first place for heaven's sake it's not like the man is a killer for sure we don't know that." It came out in one long breath without any pauses and was followed by a big gasping yawn.

"One of these days, you're going to become a morning person."

"Never."

I turned my attention back to our notes about the case.

Moira Marks—Wife of the victim. She was acting shifty on the day we talked to her. I know her pretty well thanks to her having been my wedding planner. Her behavior was definitely strange. She inherited all of her husband's money, though it wasn't much, and stood to gain the most from his death. Doesn't have an alibi.

Marcus Baron—The owner of the jewelry store. Has a bruise on his wrist but a pretty good excuse for it. Seemed to have liked Cody a lot and said he was like a son to him. Still need to get his alibi for that night.

Redford Smalls—Suspicious. Need his alibi for that night because he was the one last seen— that we know of so far—with the victim. He also ran from us when we tried to confront him.

Other clues—the victim was found inside our locked bakery. The internal alarm went off but not the external one, so how and when did he get in? He was stabbed with a knife from Bee's collection. He had my engagement ring in his hand.

And that brought us to where we were today.

I glanced at my reflection in the rearview mirror, studying myself. Jamie had a new job, and I had thought we'd put all this investigating stuff behind us. It seemed a bit extreme to be tailing a suspect, but here we were.

At some point you're going to have to start doing what feels right.

But what *was* the right thing to do?

The front door of the Carriage House opened, and Bee straightened in the driver's seat. "There he is."

I focused on our "mark."

The more I thought about him, the more suspicious I became. An out-of-towner who had been hanging around the victim before his murder. And why had they been meeting at the Claw Pot and not at Cody's home if they were friends? Would Moira have disapproved or something?

Bee and I sank low in our seats and watched the suspect approach his car—a white Honda. He got inside and drove off. Bee waited a second before tailing him. She was an expert at this type of thing by now.

We drove through Mystery, past the neatly paved sidewalks, the trees losing their leaves, growing from beds in the concrete, and through Brewer Street then up Sleuth Avenue.

Redford Smalls parked his car outside the gun store on Stock and Barrel Lane. He emerged from the car and Bee parked ours down the road, on the corner across from a florist's shop.

Redford paused on the sidewalk to look up and down the street, but if he spotted us, he didn't react.

"What is he up to?" Bee muttered.

"No idea. But it's not like he's arrived at a knife store."

"Never bring a gun to a knife murder?" Bee asked.

"But they surely sell knives in there," I said. "Don't they sell all sorts of weapons and self-defense items at places like that?"

"Doesn't matter. It was my knife that was used. Clearly, the murderer didn't plan the attack."

"Or they did," I said, "and planned on framing us."

Bee gave me close to a bewildered look. "I'm out of sleuthing practice. I didn't even consider that." She got out of the car, and we headed up the street to the gun store. We risked a quick look inside. The gun store owner—I didn't know his name but I'd seen him at the bakery a couple of times before—stood behind the counter.

Redford was nowhere to be seen.

"Where did he go?" Bee whispered. "What is he up to?"

"I wish I had an answer to either of those questions," I said.

The gun store owner didn't see us watching, but a back door opened, and Redford emerged.

He talked to the owner quietly, shaking his head, then gesturing toward the front door.

Bee and I ducked back and out of sight. "They're up to something," Bee whispered. "Why would the owner of the store allow Redford behind the counter? He doesn't work there. He's staying at the guesthouse, for heaven's sake."

Frustration built in my gut. If only we could figure out how Cody was connected to Redford —what business had they had together? And what did the gun store owner have to do with any of it?

Bee and I retreated to the car to wait, and Redford came out thirty minutes later without any packages. Again, he glanced up and down the street, didn't notice us, then promptly got into his car and drove off at high speed.

"Let's see what the owner has to say." It was the closest we'd get to information out of this reconnaissance mission of ours.

Again, we approached the gun store. The door clacked open before we reached it, and the owner emerged. He spotted us and waved his hands in our direction, flapping the air as if he could shoo us like moths. "Get out of here," he growled.

"Hello," I said. "I'm Ruby, and this is—"

"Get!" The gun store owner, his white hair lying flat against his pink head, flapped a second time. "Get out of here before I call the cops."

"Come on, Bee." I grabbed hold of my friend's arm and backed up. "It's not worth it." Jamie hadn't started work yet, obviously, but this would cause trouble.

Bee stood her ground for a second, facing down the gun store owner. "Objectionable man," she said, before marching off.

I followed her, a certainty burning through my stomach. Redford and this man had *something* to do with Cody's murder. I'd have bet my last donut that Redford had told the gun store owner not to talk to us.

We had to prove it.

Fourteen

That night late...

I TIPTOED DOWN THE HALL THAT LED TO the front door, my heart seated at the base of my throat. This wasn't the first time I'd gone sleuthing late at night, but it was certainly the first time I'd sneaked out of the house while Jamie slept. It felt devious, and I didn't like hiding things from him. But it was also necessary.

Jamie didn't need to know how close we were to finding out the truth about Cody's murder. It would only bring him extra stress. And cause discord in our relationship.

I checked that my black gloves were in place, my phone was in my pocket, and the tin of pepper spray was firmly tucked into my jeans.

A tiny meow interrupted the silence in the foyer, and I jumped.

Cookie had followed me out of my bedroom.

I bent and scratched behind his cute furry ginger ears. "Shush, darling," I whispered. "We've got to be quiet or we'll wake Jamie. Now, why don't you go lie at the end of his bed?"

Cookie purred at me then hesitated. Another small meow, if I hadn't known any better, I'd swear it was a warning, and then the ginger kitten turned and padded back down the hall. Yellow eyes peered at me through the darkness.

I let myself out into the chilly fall evening, my pulse settling now that I was out of the house.

"Finally." Bee stepped out of the darkness.

I held back a shriek, clapping my hand to my throat. "Are you trying to scare me to death?"

"Only to action," Bee replied. "You're ten minutes late."

"I don't like sneaking out of my own home," I said.

"You'll get used to it."

"Heavens, why would I do that?" I asked. "This will be the first and last time."

Bee gave me a knowing look. At least I think she did. It was dark out.

"Let's go." Bee took my arm, and we walked down the front steps together. I had parked my car further from the house tonight, under the ruse of wanting to use it early in the morning and not wanting to wake Jamie.

Really, it was for tonight. We got into it, and I tucked my phone into the pocket of my black slacks. "I don't know about this, Bee. What if we get in trouble?"

"We won't."

I started the car, my gut bubbling with nerves, and we drove off. We reached town and started toward the suburbs. Bee had got hold of

Leslie after our encounter with the gun store owner and found both his name and his address.

"It's 267 Potter Street," Bee said, "Mr. Timothy Martin."

"It would've been funny if his name was Ricky."

Bee didn't respond. She repeated the address again, and I nodded so she'd stop. It had become a mantra to her, it seemed. Maybe she also got the feeling that we were onto something. It was impossible not to feel that way after Redford's behavior.

The gun store owner, Mr. Martin, lived in a blocky house with a chain link fence. The lights were off inside, but on in the garage beside it.

"He's in there," I said. "I don't think we should do this."

"He's in the garage. This is the perfect time to snoop around." Bee exited the car and crept through the front yard, heading away from the garage and toward the side of the house.

I couldn't let her go in on her own, and she certainly wouldn't stop now that she'd set her sights on her goal.

"Oh, Bee," I whispered, before getting out of the car as quietly as I could. She had already reached the back of the house, and found an open window that looked in on an exceptionally messy bedroom.

The weirdest part about the room was the number of beds. There were three of them, all empty and unmade, sheets rumpled or pillows indented. A table pressed up against the wall was the only organized section of the bedroom.

"Come on," Bee whispered. "I'll give you a leg up." She opened the sash window all the way up, and I held my breath, praying it wouldn't make a noise or catch. It slid firmly into place with finality.

Bee bent and formed a basket with her hands. "In you go."

I placed my sneaker in the foothold she'd created for me, and she boosted me up a little. I used the momentum to clamber into the bedroom. I came down on the carpeted floor as quietly as possible. There was still a dull thump, and I held my breath, listening for the sound of approaching footsteps.

Nothing. We were clear.

I stuck my hands out the window, and Bee used them to haul herself up and inside. She'd always been admirably fit for her age—even fitter than I was, though I was twenty years her junior.

We stood in the stillness, breathing evenly.

"This place smells awful," Bee said.

And she wasn't wrong. It was like a mixture of stinky feet, rotten food, and something else I didn't care to place. "I'm going to hazard a guess that there were guys staying in here."

"And I'm going to second that guess."

We gravitated toward the table pressed up against one side of the bedroom. Papers had been stacked atop it, and a map had been tacked to the wall above the desk. No, not a map, but a blueprint. A blueprint of the jewelry store.

I sucked in a breath. "Why would they need this?"

"Look." Bee had shifted the papers on the desk to reveal several photographs of pieces from the jewelry store. One of them was the fancy jewel-encrusted watch that Mr. Baron had been working on when we'd gone to visit him.

"A heist," I breathed. "I've got to call Jamie. This is bad. We need help, Bee. These are proper robbers." I whipped my phone out of my pocket, unlocked it and started searching for his name in the contacts list on my phone.

"He's just going to be mad," Bee said, "if we call him. Come on, Ruby, we've got them cornered. I bet Cody was involved in this, and that's why they murdered him."

"Bee." But I stopped dialing Jamie's number regardless. Instead, I opened my texts and typed one out. "We're at 267 Potter Street. We think we've uncovered a jewelry heist." And then I sent it off. It wouldn't wake him, but he would know where we were if... things went badly.

"What we should do," Bee said, carefully rifling through the pictures of jewelry pieces, her black gloved fingers struggling to separate the photograph paper, "is call the police. This is enough to land them in prison. A jewelry store heist is a big deal."

She was right. Why call my fiancé when we could call the cops. "I'll call 911."

The door to the bedroom slammed open, and Mr. Martin, the gun store owner, filled the doorway. Behind him, Redford Smalls stood in the passage, glaring at us with those maleficent blue eyes.

"I'm afraid that won't be possible," Mr. Martin said through gritted teeth.

Fifteen

"RUN!" BEE YELLED, AND TRIED TO TURN tail. Mr. Martin caught her around the waist and dragged her backward.

"Bee!" I grabbed the tin of pepper spray from my pocket and lifted it. I unleashed a stream of bright red fluid from within, directing it at Mr. Martin. It hit him square in the eyes, and he let out a shriek and let go of my friend, instantly. "You don't touch her. Never."

Bee backpedaled away from him, and I made to join her but a muscular arm caught me around the shoulders and neck. Redford pulled me against his chest and held me there, not tight enough to choke, but tight enough to discourage me from trying to make an escape. He wrestled the tin of pepper spray from my grip and pointed it at Bee.

She froze, raising her hands, the palms of her black gloves a stark reminder of what we'd found and done. "I'm not going to do anything rash," she said. "Just don't hurt her. Don't hurt my friend."

"You shouldn't have come here," Redford said, over the yells of his partner in crime. "Dubbah."

"You don't say," Bee replied, but her tone was deficit of its usual bite. We were caught. Properly caught. And these weren't small town murderers, these were burly men who wanted to rob a jewelry store. And one of them owned a gun store.

I didn't see us wrestling our way out of this one.

I swallowed. "Let me go, please."

Mr. Martin writhed on the floor, hands over his eyes. Redford grunted irritably at the noise, then guided me out of the room, gesturing for

Bee to come along. "Move it, old lady," he said, "or I'll spray you."

"Old lady?" Bee grumbled it, but did as he said, her gaze darting to me constantly and the grip he had on my shoulders and neck.

"Shut up and come with me," Redford said.

He dragged us through the tiny home and into another bedroom with a double bed. He brought us inside and finally released me, then confiscated both Bee's phone and my own. Finally, he retreated to the doorway, all while Mr. Martin howled in the background.

"Don't do anything stupid," he said.

"Where are you—?"

The door slammed shut and a lock turned in the key.

Bee and I stood quietly, feet apart, staring at the exit.

Was this really happening? My mind raced.

These guys had to be the murderers, right? But if that was the case, why had Redford and Cody been meeting? Unless Cody had been in on the heist. And if they were murderers, we were in even more trouble that I'd anticipated.

Had we solved the murder and consequently doomed ourselves?

"I didn't get to call the cops," I murmured.

"We have to get out of here," Bee said, storming over to the window. She drew back the curtain—a worn piece of cotton that barely fit the name—and tried the latch. "Darn it. Locked."

I went over to join her and tugged on the bottom of the sash. I spun around, searching for something to break the window itself, but the room was empty apart from the bed and its sheets. No desk in here, no chairs or smaller items.

"The closet." Bee rushed over to it and wrenched it open, but it was empty too. "What's up with this place? Why is it so bare?"

"Must be something to do with their heist planning," I whispered, and tried the light switch. It didn't work, and the only light came from next-door's porch lights. "Bee, this is so bad. What are we going to do?"

My best friend put up a hand and shut her eyes. She took two deep breaths then turned to me. "The first thing we're going to do is not panic."

"That's something we're *not* doing," I replied. "That's the opposite of what I meant."

"You're panicking, Ruby. You need to calm down." Her voice grew shaky.

I walked over to her and placed my hands on her shoulders. "It's OK, Bee. We'll figure this out. We outnumber them. Mr. Martin is down."

The yelling outside had grown fainter, and it stopped, almost as if the gun store owner had heard me talking.

Oh no. Gun store owner. What were the chances that these men *weren't* armed? But then why would they have stabbed Cody?

I shook my head, trying to clear it of the extraneous thoughts.

"Do you have a bobby pin?" I asked. "We can pick the lock." Bee had a particular set of skills—they included baking, sleuthing, and lock-picking. And a surprisingly strong throwing arm, especially when she was lobbing baked goods at her enemies.

"No," she said. "Do you?"

"No, but if we can find something similar,

we can pick the lock on the window and get out of here before they—"

A key turned in the door lock, and a man entered the room. A thatch of curly hair was seated against his skull, and he smiled at us, his mouth crooked, his clothes similarly skew and—

A shock of recognition nearly knocked me back a step. This was the guy! The strange, creepy guy who'd given me back my ring at the beginning of the week. The one that walked like a turtle.

"You," I cried, throwing out an arm in front of Bee. "What are you doing here?"

Redford appeared behind the "turtle" man. "You know them, Gunther?"

The newcomer froze then turned his head, neck still sticking out strangely. "You've been using your real names in front of these women?"

Redford had the decency to look abashed.

"Idiots," Gunther said, before turning back toward us. "I see you've found us, Miss Holmes. Miss Pine."

"Who are you?" Bee demanded. "You're not from around here."

"Don't worry about who I am. Worry about

what's going to happen next." Gunther entered the room with us.

Bee and I shuffled backward as one. I found her hand in the half-gloom.

"Back off," Bee said. "You stay away from us."

"Or what?" Gunther asked.

"Or we'll…"

Gunther gave me a sardonic look. "Yes?"

Silence.

"That's what I thought. You'll do nothing except exactly what I say. You two have managed to uncover a plot that has taken years to come together. We are mere hours away from executing it, and you're not going to stop us now."

"We won't tell anyone," I said.

Bee squeezed my hand. She knew it was pointless to argue with these men. They wouldn't let us go.

"You're right," Gunther replied, coming ever closer. "You're not going to tell anyone. Because you're not going to live to tell the tale."

"I don't like the idea of leaving bodies behind," Redford said from behind him. "I don't like—"

"Shut up," Gunther snarled. "Your opinion doesn't matter. You're here to hack the alarm system and nothing else, and if you—"

A thundering bang came from the front door, followed by boot-heels. Redford let out an alarmed yell and stepped into the hall. A police officer, clad in a bulletproof vest and helmet, tackled him to the ground. Another officer ran in, yelling instructions, pointing a gun directly at Gunther.

The snarl disappeared from Gunther's face. In fact, it went entirely blank. He put up his hands and turned toward the officers, complying with their instructions.

Bee and I did the same thing in case we were considered suspects as well. A brief burst of panic was followed by relief. The police were here. We were saved. And the real murderers had been arrested.

Sixteen

"ARE YOU SURE YOU DON'T WANT anything else, Miss Pine?" Detective Winters had positioned himself across from me in the gray interrogation room. He uncapped his bottle of water and took a sip before setting it back on the steel table. "I can get you a coffee. It's not good coffee, but it's passable. It'll give you a boost."

"I'm fine," I said. "I don't think I need a boost of anything. I'm not even sure I'll sleep again." My teeth chattered occasionally though I wasn't cold. I figured it was part of the shock of what had happened.

Bee and I had helped bring down a gang of

jewelry store robbers. I reeled to piece the details together.

It was my text—the gut feeling I'd had about danger had been right—to Jamie that had saved us. He'd woken to the sound of the message and had alerted the cops immediately.

"I think you'd better tell me everything you know," Detective Winters said sternly, the grittiness of his voice more pronounced late at night. Maybe he'd been pulled from his bed, half-asleep, to come in and question us and the robbers.

"I already gave my statement," I said. "And Bee has too. We weren't involved in any of this. Not in Cody's murder or the plan to rob the jewelry store next-door to our bakery."

Detective Winters considered me, and I couldn't read his expression. "You think Cody Marks was involved in the heist?"

"It's the only thing that makes sense," I said, fiddling with my water bottle. "Think about it. Cody and Redford were the last people seen together before his murder. They were sighted at the Claw Pot at 07:30 p.m.. Why would they have been meeting unless it was in relation to the heist. Cody had access to the jewelry store. He was probably the inside man, while Redford was meant to hack the alarm system. That Gunther guy said so while he was threatening us."

Detective Winters made notes while I talked.

It felt good to say it out loud. "And then there's Mr. Martin from the gun store. He was involved too, and I bet it was so that they would have the necessary fire power they needed in case things went wrong."

"Where did Gunther come into it?" Detective Winters asked.

"He was the mastermind, I guess. He acted like the one in charge when they captured us, but I'm not sure how he fits into the group. Mr. Martin lives in town, right? And Redford had been visiting Cody frequently, so he must have been a distant friend or some connection Cody had met somewhere down the line, but Gunther... I don't know." I paused and took a sip of water, working the moisture around my mouth before swallowing.

"Do you know Gunther's full name?" Detective Winters held the nib of his pen above the page of his notepad.

"No," I said. "I've only ever seen him twice, and the first time he didn't introduce himself."

"His name is Gunther Baron."

I sucked in a sharp breath. "Baron? As in Marcus Baron, the jewelry store owner?"

"Correct. Gunther is Marcus' son."

A memory of that day in the jewelry store came back to me. I'd gone in to get my ring re-sized, right after Gunther had given it back to me, and Marcus had gotten a phone call from his son. It sounded like they were about to have an argument. And hadn't Marcus said something like his son never visited or didn't help? I couldn't quite recall.

"Then that's how he fits in," I whispered. "Goodness, I can't believe that. It's horrible. Why would you want to rob your own father?"

"Gunther's an interesting man," Detective Winters said easily. "He's got a history of breaking the law. Wanted in a few states."

"Wow." I hadn't even thought about re-searching Marcus Baron or his family. We'd been so focused on Redford, Moira, and the connec-tions between them all that it hadn't occurred to Bee and me to check him out in such detail. But that was fine. The case was closed. "I'm glad it's all over. Cody's murder is solved, and the culprits are behind bars."

Detective Winters cleared his throat. "Unfortunately not."

"Huh?" My jaw went slack. "What do you mean?"

"Gunther Baron didn't kill Cody," Detective Winters said. "Neither did Redford Smalls. Or Timothy Martin."

"What? They didn't?"

"They didn't," Detective Winters said. "They have alibis for that night. Gunther was photographed at a local ATM at the time of the murder. Redford was with a friend at a local bar. Timothy Martin wasn't in town that night, but was at a gun enthusiast's convention the town over."

I swallowed. "Why are you telling me this?"

"Because all of these men were seen by multiple people in public places or caught on camera at the time of the murder," Detective Winters. "They planned on robbing the jewelry store, yes, and they'll be charged for that. Not for murder."

"But that doesn't make sense," I said.

"There's no one else it could be. Unless it was Moira or Marcus himself, or Marcus' wife? Or..."

"You," Detective Winters said. "And your friend."

"We were with my fiancé at the time of the murder."

"When was the time of the murder?" Detective Winters asked, leaning forward.

"Sometime between 07:30 p.m. and 08:00 p.m.," I replied. "That's when Redford was last seen with Cody at the Claw Pot. And we got the call from the alarm company at—"

"You seem well versed in what's going on with this case," Winters said. "Why is that?"

"Because you're accusing me of being something I'm not," I said firmly.

Winters narrowed his eyes at me.

I lifted my chin, trying to be defiant even though I couldn't believe what I'd heard tonight. The men weren't the killers, and there had been a jewelry store heist about to take place right next door. "Am I under arrest?" I asked.

"Not yet," Winters said. "You're free to go.

And you're free to return to your bakery. The scene has been released and cleaned."

I rose from the chair, abandoning my water bottle on the table, and left the room without another word. I walked down the hall—it was my second time here, so I didn't need any guidance—and out into a room full of arranged desks and officers seated at them. The receptionist eyed me as I passed her position and exited through the old wooden door of the police station.

Jamie waited at the base of the steps outside, the light from a nearby by lamppost casting him in silhouette. His hands were clenched into fists at his sides.

"Honey," I said. "Thank you for coming, I—"

"Ruby." He was stiff as a board, his frown deep. "Why are you doing this again?"

"Doing what?"

"Investigating murders? I thought you two got this out of your system."

"What?" I could barely believe my ears. Jamie knew us by now. Heck, part of the reason I'd agreed to get engaged to him was because he accepted both Bee and me for who we were. We liked to figure things out, especially if they affected our business.

I walked down the stairs to join him. "You said that you—"

"I know what I said." He moved out of my reach.

"Then why are you mad about this?"

"I'm picking you up from the police station," he said. "In our new home town. In the dead of the night. A week before I start working here. Don't you see the problem with this scenario?"

"Yes, I get that, really I do, but—"

"I don't think you get it, Ruby. And I don't think we should continue planning our wedding until you think about this."

"About what?"

"What you want our lives to be like in this town," Jamie said, before turning on his heel and walking off.

"This isn't fair," I shouted, my voice hitching in my throat. "I thought you understood who I am. Who I—"

But Jamie was already gone.

Seventeen

The following morning...

THE BAKERY SMELLED STRONGLY OF chemicals—the stuff they had used to clean up the crime scene—and was as quiet as the darkened street outside. I grasped the back of one of the chairs, stroking the back of my bare ring finger with my thumb and trying to make sense of the last twelve hours.

Jamie had waited for Bee and me in his Jeep Grand Wagoneer. We had driven home together in utter silence. I hadn't slept a wink all night long, even though Cookie had done his best to comfort me with his purring cuteness.

Five hours later, I had woken and come to the bakery alone, hoping to clean up the place, but all I'd done for the last fifteen minutes was stand and stare in sullen silence.

Jamie was furious. He had said things he couldn't take back. And I couldn't figure out where we were headed.

Or what had happened to Cody. That still played on my mind because as much as I would've liked to promise I'd never investigate a crime again, I couldn't do that. No. I wouldn't do that.

What if that meant losing Jamie and everything we'd started building here in Mystery?

Trust your gut. What do you want?

I swallowed, tears building in the corners of my eyes.

What I wanted was for life to be normal. What I wanted was to understand how Cody had wound up in the bakery. And who had murdered him.

A knock rattled the glass front door, and I gasped.

A figure stood outside, swathed in a thick black coat, pale face peering into the bakery. Moira, my wedding planner, her lips turned ever downward at the corners, gestured for me to let her in.

I walked over to the door and placed my hand on the lock.

What if she's the murderer?

I let her in, stepping back so she could enter.

"Ruby," she groaned, in her usual morose tone. "Oh, Ruby. We have to talk. We have to talk right now." Moira rushed over to one of the seats and dropped into it.

I locked the door then joined her. "Moira? What's wrong? You look shaken up?"

"That's cause I am shaken up," she said, shivering. "My shoulders are tighter than bark on a tree. I don't think I've ever been this afraid."

"Would you like a cup of coffee?" I didn't have anything baked or ready to go since the bakery had been out of commission for a while, but I could do a black coffee.

"No. No, thank you," Moira replied. "But I need your help."

"Why? How?"

Moira gulped. "I don't know if you've heard the news, but Redford Smalls has been arrested. He's being charged with murder and burglary."

I opened my mouth to correct her but then thought better of it. Why would Moira care what happened to Redford? Unless...

"I know that you're the only one who can fix this because I—Well, I—"

"What is it, Moira?"

"You're my friend, right, Ruby?" Moira asked.

"I—"

"We've been working together for a while," she continued. "I would consider you a friend. I didn't know who else to turn to."

I frowned. "Moira, what are you—?"

"I need you to tell Detective Winters that you were with Redford on the night of the murder," Moira said. "Please. You have to make up something."

"Huh?" This was getting stranger by the second. "Why would I do that?"

"Because..." Moira covered her face with both hands. "Because I was with Redford on the night Cody was murdered. I was with him, and I —well, I was in love with him. I *am* in love with him. But if the police know that, they'll think I'm the one who murdered my husband. But I didn't. I swear. I was with Redford."

"But if you were with Redford," I said, "then you have an alibi, Moira."

"Yes, but what will the people of Mystery think?" Moira asked. "I'm supposed to be a wedding planner. I was meant to be the one with the happy marriage. With everything figured out. If they think I'm a fraud, I'll never work again."

"I don't know about that."

Moira's hand snaked out and caught my wrist. "Please. You have to help me. I can't stand the thought of anything happening to Redford, and I can't lose my business. It's the only thing I have left."

I tried not to show my disbelief. How could she ask this of me? Sure, Redford wasn't technically in trouble for murder—Detective Winters had told me as much—but Moria clearly thought so. And she was willing to sacrifice my reputation to protect her own.

"Moira, you know I'm engaged," I said. "I can't say I was with another man on the night of—"

"You're not even wearing your ring," Moira replied. "I thought you'd called it off. Besides, that fiancé of yours is never with you. He's always off at different—"

I rose from the chair, shrugging her off. "Redford hasn't been arraigned for Cody's murder," I said stiffly. "He was arrested for conspiring to rob the jewelry store next-door. That's it. That's all. So, you don't need to tell anyone he was with you. Although, it might be a good idea to tell the police your alibi so they don't charge you with Cody's murder." I left her sitting stunned at the table and went to open the bakery door. I held it for her.

A cold breeze swept into the bakery, swirling through the chemical scent.

Moira came to her senses rapidly. She wrapped her dark coat around her body and stepped out into the early morning darkness.

"Ruby, please," she said. "Please forgive me. I was desperate. I—"

I closed the door then walked through the bakery proper and into the kitchen. I stood among the steel counters, trying to collect my thoughts.

Moira was innocent. A horrible person, apparently, but innocent.

Who did that leave?

I shivered in the chill in the kitchen then turned on the oven for when Bee would arrive to make the baked donuts.

All the conspirators involved in the jewelry store heist were innocent. Moira, who had stood to gain the most out of Cody's passing, was innocent. Who did that leave?

Marcus Baron.

But why? And how?

And how on earth could I prove it?

Eighteen

"HEAVENS TO MURGATROYD," BEE SAID, as she entered the kitchen. "It's colder than a witch's stare in here."

"Huh?" I turned around, trying to bring my thoughts back to the present. Once again, I'd been lost in considering the case. I wasn't sure how long it had been since Moira had dropped by for her visit, but light had started filtering into the alley outside, visible through the closed kitchen window, turning it from black to a dull gray.

"How are you, Ruby?" Bee placed an arm

around my shoulders. She stifled a yawn. "Did you get any sleep?"

"Barely."

"Jamie?"

"Yeah. And the case," I said. "There's something weird going on here."

"How so?" Bee checked the settings on the oven then rubbed her arms. "Why is it so darn cold? Have you checked the thermostat?"

"No."

Bee strode over to it while I filled her in on what had happened with Moira. Hearing myself say it out loud didn't help make the case any clearer. We didn't have the right evidence. We didn't know how Cody had wound up in the bakery. Or why he'd been holding my ring—unless it was part of the heist plan or he'd been working on it at the time. "Or," I said, "how the murderer got in and out of the bakery before and after the murder."

"This is weird," Bee said.

"Right? I mean, that only leaves Marcus Baron as the suspect."

"Not what I'm talking about." Bee tapped the thermostat. "It's set to the correct temperature, but it's struggling to get up there. It's like there's a—" Her eyes widened. "Wait a minute."

"What?"

Bee tapped her chin. "Hmm."

"What is it? Bee?"

"Remember at the beginning of the week when Leslie was complaining about her bread dough?"

"Sure. But what's that got to do with anything?"

"She kept saying that she's never had problems with rising dough before," Bee continued, "and that things had been weird for the last two weeks."

"OK?"

"And right now it's cold in here," Bee said. "The temperature isn't being regulated correctly."

"I'm still not following."

"So, bread dough struggles to rise when there isn't enough warmth," Bee said.

"Yeah?"

Bee clicked her fingers. "Which means there's a leak."

"I still don't get it."

"Come over here," Bee said.

I went over to the thermostat. "What is it?"

"See that little flashing indicator on the screen? That means there's a leak and the thermostat is struggling to regulate it. Where does Leslie usually leave the bread to rise?"

"In the pantry," I said.

"Exactly." Bee walked over to the pantry door and bent in front of it. She placed her fingers near the crack between the wood and the neatly tiled floor. "Come feel this."

I bent beside her and extended my hand. A soft but cold breeze drifted from under the door. Which didn't make any sense, since there weren't any windows in the pantry. The door rattled softly, and I swallowed, meeting my friend's gaze.

Bee's hazel eyes were alive with excitement. She straightened and opened the pantry door, hurriedly. The shelves looked exactly as we'd left them—organized and clearly marked, nothing out of place or expired. We ran our business like professionals. After all that time on the food truck, it was a luxury to have this much space.

Bee and I walked down the long aisle that led between the shelves and racks and—

A dog barked loudly to our right.

I froze, finding Bee's arm and squeezing. I pointed to the wall behind the rack. It was the same slate color as the rest of the room, but there was something off about it. It was... "Moving," I whispered.

A dog yipped again, coming from the other side of that "moving" wall.

"Help me with this," Bee whispered, gesturing to the steel rack. Thankfully, it wasn't densely packed with Tupperware or dried goods. We shifted them off and stacked them at record speed, then moved the rack to one side, so we'd have access to the strange section of wall.

Bee stepped up to it and put out her hand. She drew it back instantly, beckoning to me. "The breeze," she mouthed.

I moved over to feel it. She was right. The breeze we'd felt, icy cold, with the nip of an early fall morning, came straight through that section of wall. But how?

I pressed my hand to what should have been

smooth concrete and it depressed inward. "Some kind of cardboard," I murmured.

Again, a dog barked. It sounded like a small dog, and it was definitely coming from the other side of the *fake* wall.

"Shush," a woman whispered. "Someone's going to hear you, Dopey." The voice was vaguely familiar.

Bee gave me the "look" before stepping forward, forming a fist, and punching the wall. Her fist went right through the cardboard. Together, we started ripping and tearing our way through to reveal... a jagged hole that led from the pantry, into a brightly lit office.

The tableau was like something out of a movie.

Us standing in the pantry, beside a ragged hole, peering through into what could only be the jewelry store's office, where a woman wearing beige stood crouched next to an open safe, grasping handfuls of dollars.

The dog barked again, going wild at the sight of us, and the woman let out a soft gasping shriek.

I recognized her. She was Marcus Baron's

wife. The timid-looking woman we'd seen in the store earlier in the week, waiting for him to finish work.

"Well," Bee said, "I think we've solved the mystery of how Cody got into the bakery."

Nineteen

BEE SCRAMBLED THROUGH THE HOLE
and into the jewelry store office. I followed her,
my gut telling me that it was safe to do so. The
jewelry store owner's wife, I couldn't remember
her name for the life of me, didn't seem danger-
ous. She trembled at the sight of us, and her dog,
who looked a lot like her, shivered in her arms.

"Wait," she said. "You don't understand.
Please."

"What's your name?" I asked. "You're Marcus' wife, right?"

She nodded, glancing at an open window,
high up on the wall. That explained where the

breeze had been coming from. No wonder poor Leslie's dough had flopped. Every time Marcus opened a window, it would come through.

I peered at the other side of the hole—in the office—with a critical eye. It looked like there had been an equally convincing section of cardboard pasted over this side at one point. But someone had ripped it off.

"What's your name?" Bee had lost her patience. Now was the time for answers.

"Julia Baron," she said, her voice matching her tiny frame. "I didn't kill Cody."

The statement rang in the small space.

"And I didn't rip the cardboard off the wall. I didn't even know it was like this until tonight." She set down the piles of cash on top of the desk and shifted her dog, Dopey, to her other arm.

Bee lifted her phone from her pocket and held it aloft, showing off Detective Winters name and number on the screen. "You'd better start talking."

"I'm just here to get the money and leave," she said. "I'm going to bail out my son. Gunther. They've accused him of—I'm going to bail him out. I—"

"That's a lot of money," I said. "Is that *all* you're going to do?"

"I was going to take him away," Julia admitted, lifting her head. A hint of defiance had entered her dark eyes. "I—I wanted to get him away from Marcus. I wanted to save him before he did—before he k-killed him." It clearly took a lot of effort for her to say it out loud.

"Marcus? Marcus killed Cody?" I asked. "You're sure?"

"Yes," Julia said. "For the past month, Marcus has been acting strangely. He's been coming to work at strange hours of the day, examining the jewelry. He's been talking about how the jewelry quality isn't what it should be, that he's sure some of the diamonds have been replaced or that Cody was making shortcuts."

That explained why my ring needed resizing.

"As time passed, he became increasingly convinced that Cody was stealing from him. He started asking questions. Making us go to the same restaurants as Cody. Following him around. And then..." She gulped, and Dopey's trembling increased tenfold, like he could sense his owner's unease. "And then, about a week ago, he came home and told me that Cody was planning to steal from the jewelry store. He wasn't sure when or how, but he knew there was going to be a heist."

"What happened?"

"The night that Cody... The night *it* happened, Marcus told me he was going to be working late. Real late. But when he came home that night, I was still awake. I was in bed, but I heard him come in. He went to the bathroom and took a shower. He doesn't usually do that." Tears swam in Julia's eyes. "The next morning, I found his clothes from the previous night in the trash can. They were covered in blood."

I gasped.

"I—I just want to get out of here. I want to run away. Marcus knows that Gunther was involved. He'll kill him next!"

"Have you gone to the police?" Bee asked.

Julia let out a gasp. "Marcus will find out. He'll know that I did it and then he'll kill me next."

"He won't be able to if he's behind bars," Bee replied, in a tone that said Julia was dumb for thinking otherwise.

"Where are the clothes, Julia?" I asked. "What did you do with the clothes he threw away?"

She licked her lips. "I stashed them in the cellar."

"And where's Marcus?" Bee asked.

"He's at home. Asleep. He's been sleeping better now that Cody's gone. But he was furious when he found out that Gunther was in town. And that he's responsible for what's been going on at the jewelry store."

Marcus must have found the hole that led from the jewelry store to the bakery. Likely, it had been the escape route for the robbers, especially since they'd had Redford, the IT specialist, to deal with the alarm systems. But when Marcus had come to confront Cody that night, Redford hadn't been around.

I could picture it now, Marcus arriving, Cody running from him, and Marcus following into the bakery. The stabbing. The death and then Marcus' hasty retreat. It added up.

"—I can't do that," Julia said. "He'll find out."

Bee walked toward the office door and

locked it, placing herself between Julia and the exited. Dopey let out a barking growl of alarm. "I'm calling Detective Winters right now. Either you tell him or we do. And if we do, he'll arrest you and charge you for withholding information. You're an accessory to murder if you don't cooperate." I wasn't sure if that was true or if Bee was trying to scare her.

I quickly moved into place in front of the hole that led back through the bakery.

"You'd better make up your mind, Julia," Bee said. "Your husband will wake up soon."

Slowly, Julia looked from me to Bee and then back again. Finally, she nodded. "I'll talk. If you really believe the cops can protect me, then I'll talk."

Bee broke out a smile. She lifted her phone and hit a button. "Detective Winters?"

"Miss Pine," he said, sounded grumpy through the loudspeaker.

"I suggest you come down to the bakery at once," Bee said. "We've got new evidence that will lead to the arrest of Cody Marks' murderer."

"What?" The sound of Winters shuffling upright in bed.

I could tell Bee was relishing this. He'd also questioned her thoroughly, and she hated being bossed around. "You heard me correctly," Bee said. "We've got new evidence that will lead to an arrest. Please come to the bakery. The front door is unlocked. Once you're inside, come through the kitchen, into the pantry, and through the hole in the wall. We're waiting for you."

"Is this some kind of prank call?" Detective Winters asked. "Because if it is—"

"Do I strike you as the type of woman who places prank calls?" Bee snapped.

"Fair enough." And then Winters hung up.

Bee lowered her phone, still smiling. I felt a little whoop of victory. Once Detective Winters got here, it wouldn't be long until Marcus was arrested, and the evidence linking him to the crime scene was found.

We'd done it again. We'd solved another case —this time by trusting our instincts.

Twenty

Five days later...

"THANK YOU FOR YOUR PATRONAGE," I said, handing over the box from behind the counter in Bee's Bakery. "Have a delightful day."

Gracie, a new mother with a baby on her hip, gave me a broad grin in return before leaving the bakery with her box. She'd ordered a dozen assorted donuts, some baked and some fried, as she did every week.

The morning rush had ended at last, and it

was past time for my break. The local newspaper, *The Mystery Mail*, lay on a nearby table, folded neatly in half to show off the headline of the week.

Bakers Solve Impossible Crime! Police Chief to Award Medals!

My heart leaped in my chest. After our discussion with Detective Winters last week, Marcus had been arrested and charged with first degree murder. Julia had opted not to bail out her son after realizing she didn't have enough money for it. And Bee and I had expected the worst.

We'd envisioned the local newspaper running a feature about us being interferers—that had happened before in other small towns—or that we'd get in trouble with Winters.

But no, Detective Winters had been delighted that we'd helped him. Apparently, the lack of physical evidence—the knife hadn't had any DNA or fingerprints on it, other than the victim's—had made the case nearly impossible to solve.

They'd been close after the arrest of the heist

members, but not close enough. And we'd helped set the final puzzle piece in place.

I made myself a coffee at the coffee station, trying not to think about my fiancé.

Jamie and I hadn't talked since his outburst at the police station. And it made for awkward dinners and breakfasts. I still didn't have my ring back, and at this point, I was starting to wonder if he wanted me to have it at all.

The bakery door opened, and I looked up, expecting a customer.

Jamie stood just inside the door. "Hi," he said.

"Hello."

"I'm a coward," he said. "And selfish."

"OK."

He strode forward. "I was jealous."

I didn't know what to say to that.

"I was jealous that you and Bee were investigating a mystery without me, even though I was so wrapped up in my own business, Ruby. I wanted desperately to impress you. I guess, a part of my ego was challenged because you two have this amazing gift. This talent. Not only are you successful business owners, but you're fantastic sleuths too. You're better at investigating cases than I was when I was a detective. And it hurts sometimes."

I held back anger, but my frown came through regardless.

"I know," he said, waving a hand. "I know. You have every right to be angry at me because it's not your problem that I'm not as accomplished as you are. It's mine. I should not have taken that out on you. I should not have acted like such a..." He searched for the right words.

"It's fine," I said. "Well, it's not. But I get it now. Thanks for explaining."

"I should be happy for you two, and I'm just jealous. I'm like an accessory to your life rather than an integral part of it, and I guess I need to find my feet," he said.

"So, we're breaking up then?" Numbness cascaded over me. This couldn't be happening, could it? What was I going to do? We'd just moved in together. To a brand new town. Everything had been going great until—

"No! What? Never. I'm madly in love with you," Jamie said. "I never want to break up with you. I—I'm saying that I can't go back in time and change things. So I'm not going to accept the position at the police department."

"What? But Jamie, I—!"

"I realized that it's not what I want to do," Jamie said. "I realized that I don't know what I want to do yet, and that's OK. We have money, and I have time to figure it out. I don't know, maybe I'll end up writing a book about you and Bee." He laughed at himself. "I don't want anything to come between us ever again. I love you. I don't want to ruin what we have because I have ego issues about not being successful."

"But you are successful," I said.

"Ruby, come on," he replied. "I inherited my money. It's not like I started a tech company or something and sold it. I'm finding myself. I have to ask that you'll have patience with me while I go through this process."

I circled the counter and went over to him, taking both his tan, callused hands in mine. "Of course, I will. I love you. And I accept your apology."

"Thank you," he replied.

We hugged, and Jamie pressed a kiss to my forehead. The stress that had gathered in my shoulders and back over the past week finally released, and I could enjoy the moment. He smelled of that earthy green cologne I loved and sea salt from the bay.

"Oh," he said, pulling back and opening his palm, "and I think you dropped this by the way."

An engagement ring, the original one he'd bought me when he'd first proposed, sat in the center of his palm. He slipped it onto my ring finger, and I was pleased to discover it fit perfectly.

I fiddled with it, smiling. "It's not going anywhere."

"And neither am I," he replied.

"Good." Together, we sat down at one of the tables to have a cup of coffee. Bee emerged from the kitchen and came over to join us, relief written all over her features as she took her seat.

"You know," she said, "I've been thinking about the bakery's name."

"What about it?" I asked.

"I figured we should rebrand," she said.

"Rebrand? To what?"

Bee flashed me her gap-toothed grin. "The

Hole in the Wall Bakery. They can grab a donut and a fistful of diamonds with every order."

We burst out laughing, and the sound of it traveled through the bakery, filling it with the joy that I'd always hoped but never dreamed would permeate my life.

Ruby and Bee's adventures continue in the second book in A Bee's Bakery Cozy Mystery series. *You can grab* Death by Cookie Dough *by clicking here!*

Craving More Cozy Mystery?

If you had fun with Ruby and Bee, you'll, love getting to know Charlie Mission and her butt-kicking grandmother, Georgina. You can read the first chapter of Charlie's story, *The Case of the Waffling Warrants,* below!

"Come in, Big G, come in." I spoke under my breath so that the flesh-colored microphone seated against my throat picked up my voice. "What is your status?"

My grandmother, Georgina—pet name

Gamma, code name Big G—was out on a special operation. Reconnaissance at the newest guest-house in our town, Gossip. The reason? First, she was an ex-spy, as was I, and second, the woman who'd opened the guesthouse was her mortal enemy and in direct competition with my grandmother's establishment, the Gossip Inn.

Who was this enemy, this bringer of potential financial doom?

A middle-aged woman with a penchant for wearing pashminas and annoying anyone who looked her way.

Jessie Belle-Blue.

It was rumored that even thinking the woman's name summoned a murder of crows.

"I repeat, Big G, what is your status?"

"I'm en route to the nest," my grandmother replied in my earpiece.

I let out a relieved sigh and exited my bedroom, heading downstairs to help with the breakfast service.

In the nine months since I had retired as a spy, life in Gossip had been normal. In the Gossip sense of the term. I'd expected that my job as a server, maid, and assistant would bring the usual level of "cat herding" inherent when working at the inn. Whether that involved tracking down runaway cats, literally, or providing a guest with a moist towelette after a fainting spell—tempers ran high in Gossip.

What was the reason for the craziness? Shoot, it had to be something in the water.

I took the main stairs two at a time and found my friend, the inn's chef, paging through her recipe book in the lime green kitchen. Lauren Harris wore her red hair in a French braid today, apron stretched over her pregnant belly.

"Morning," I said, "how are you today?"

"Madder than a fat cat on a diet." She slapped her recipe book closed and turned to me.

Uh oh. Looks like it's time for more cat herding.

"What's wrong?"

"My supplier is out of flour and sugar. Can you believe that?" Lauren huffed, smoothing her hands over her belly while the clock on the wall ticked away. Breakfast was in two hours and Lauren loved baking cupcakes as part of the meal.

"Do you have enough supplies to make cupcakes for this morning?"

"Yes. But just for today," Lauren replied. "The guests are going to love my new waffle cupcakes, and they'll be sore they can't get anymore after this batch is done. Why, I should go down there and wring Billy's neck for doing this to me. He knows I take an order of sugar and flour every week, and I get it at just above cost too. What's Georgina going to say?"

"Don't stress, Lauren," I said. "We'll figure it out."

"Right." She brightened a little. "I nearly forgot you're the one who "fixes" things around here." Lauren winked at me.

She was the only person in the entire town who knew that my grandmother and I had once been spies for the NSIB—the National Security Investigative Bureau. But the news that I had helped solve several murders had spread through town, and now, anybody and everybody with a problem would call me up asking for help. A lot of them offered me money. And I was selective about who I chose to help.

"I'll check it out for you if you'd like," I said. "The flour issue."

"Nah, that's OK. I'm sure Billy will get more stock this week. I'll lean on him until he squeals."

"Sounds like you've been picking up tips from Georgina."

Lauren giggled then returned to her super-secret recipe book—no one but she was allowed to touch it.

"What's on the menu this morning?" I asked.

Lauren was the boss in the kitchen—she told me what to do, and I followed her instructions precisely. If I did anything else, like trying to read the recipe for instance, the food would end up burned, missing ingredients or worse.

The only place I wasn't a "fixer" was in the Gossip Inn's kitchen.

"Bacon and eggs over easy, biscuits and gravy, waffle cupcakes and... oh, I can't make fresh baked bread, can I?"

"Tell her I'll bring some back with me from

the bakery." Gamma's voice startled me. Goodness, I'd forgotten about the earpiece—she could hear everything happening in the kitchen.

"I'll text Georgina and ask her to bring bread from the bakery."

"You're a lifesaver, Charlotte."

We set to work on the breakfast—it was 7:00 a.m. and we needed everything done within two hours—and fell into our easy rhythm of baking and cooking.

My grandmother entered the kitchen at around 8:30 a.m., dressed in a neat silk blouse and a pair of slacks rather than the black outfit she'd left in for her spy mission. Tall, willowy, and with neatly styled gray hair, Gamma had always reminded me of Helen Mirren playing the Queen.

"Good morning, ladies," she said, in her prim, British accent. "I bring bread and tidings."

"What did you find out?" I asked.

"No evidence of the supposed ghost tours," Gamma said.

We'd started hosting ghost tours at the inn recently, so of course Jessie Belle-Blue wanted to do the same. She was all about under-cutting us, but, thankfully, the Gossip Inn had a legacy and over 1,000 positive reviews on TripAdvisor.

Breakfast time arrived, and the guests filled the quaint dining area with its glossy tables, creaking wooden floors, and egg yolk yellow walls. Chatter and laughter leaked through the swinging kitchen doors with their porthole windows.

"That's my cue," I said, dusting off my apron, and heading out into the dining room.

I picked up a pot of coffee from the sideboard where we kept the drinks station and started my rounds.

Most of the guests had gathered around a center table in the dining room, and bursts of laughter came from the group, accompanied by the occasional shout.

I elbowed my way past a couple of guests—nobody could accuse me of having great people skills—apologizing along the way until I reached the table. The last time something like this had happened, a murder had followed shortly afterward.

Not this time. No way.

"—the last thing she'd ever hear!" The woman seated at the table, drawing the attention, was vaguely familiar. She wore her dark hair in luscious curls, and tossed it as she spoke, looking down her upturned nose at the people around the table.

"What happened then, Mandy?" Another woman asked, her hands clasped together in front of her stomach.

Mandy? Wait a second, isn't this Mandy Gilmore?

Gamma had mentioned her once before—Mandy was a massive gossip in town. Why wasn't she staying at her house?

"What happened? Well, she ran off with her tail between her legs, of course. She'll soon learn not to cross me. Heaven knows, I always repay my debts."

"What, like a Lannister from *Game of Thrones*?" That had come from a taller woman with ginger curls.

"Shut up, Opal," Mandy replied. "You have no idea what we're talking about, and even if you did, you wouldn't have the intelligence to comprehend it."

The crowd let out various 'oofs' in response to that. The woman next to me clapped her hand over her mouth.

"You're all talk, Gilmore." Opal lifted a hand and yammered it at the other woman. "You act like you're a threat, but we know the truth around here."

"The truth?" Mandy leaned in, pressing her hands flat onto the tabletop, the crystal vase in the center rattling. "And what's that, Opal, darling? I'd love to hear it."

"That you're a failure. You sold your house, left Gossip with your head in the clouds, told everyone you were going to become a successful businesswoman, and now you're back. Back to scrape together the pieces of the life you have left."

"Witch!" Mandy scraped her chair back.

"All right, all right," I said, setting down the coffee pot on the table. "That's enough, ladies. Everyone head back to their tables before things get out of hand."

Both Opal and Mandy stared daggers at me.

I flashed them both smiles. "We wouldn't want to ruin breakfast, would we? Lauren's prepared waffle cupcakes."

That distracted them. "Waffle cupcakes?" Opal's brow wrinkled. "How's that going to work?"

"Let's talk about it at your table." I grabbed my coffee pot and walked her away from Mandy. The crowd slowly dispersed, people muttering regret at having missed out on a show. The Gossip Inn was popular for its constant conflict.

If the rumors didn't start here then they weren't worth repeating. That was the mantra, anyway.

I seated Opal at her table, and she pursed her lips at me. "You shouldn't have interrupted. That woman needs a piece of my mind."

"We prefer peace of mind at the inn." I put up another of my best smiles.

Compared to what I'd been through in the past—hiding out from my rogue spy ex-husband and eventually helping put him behind bars when he found me—dealing with the guests was a cakewalk.

"What brings you to Gossip, Opal?" I asked.

"I live here," she replied, waspishly. "I'm staying here while they're fumigating my house. Roaches."

"Ah." I struggled not to grimace. Thankfully, my cell phone buzzed in the front pocket of my apron and distracted me. "Coffee?"

"I don't take caffeine." And she said it like I'd offered her an illegal substance too.

"Call me if you need anything." I hurried off before she could make good on that promise, bringing my phone out of my pocket.

I left the coffee pot on the sideboard, moving into the Gossip Inn's spacious foyer, the chandelier overhead off, but catching light in glimmers. The tables lining the hall were filled with trinkets from the days when the inn had been a museum—an eclectic collection of bits and bobs.

"This is Charlotte Smith," I answered the call—I would never get to use my true last name, Mission, again, but it was safer this way.

"Hello, Charlotte." A soft, rasping voice. "I've been trying to get through to you. I'm desperate."

"Who is this?"

"My name is Tina Rogers, and I need your help."

"My help."

"Yes," she said. "I understand that you have a certain set of skills. That you fix people's problems?"

"I do. But it depends on the problem and the price." I didn't have a set fee for helping people, but if it drew me away from the inn for long, I had to charge. I was technically a consultant now. Sort of like a P.I. without the fedora and coffee-stained shirt.

"My mother will handle your fee," Tina said. "I've asked her to text you about it, but I... I don't have long to talk. They're going to pull me off the phone soon."

"Who?"

"The police," she replied. "I'm calling you from the holding cell at the Gossip Police Station. I've been arrested on false charges, and I need you to help me prove my innocence."

"Miss Rogers, it's probably a better idea to invest in a lawyer." But I was tempted. It had been a long time since I'd felt useful.

"No! I'm not going to a lawyer. I'm going to

make these idiots pay for ever having arrested me."

I took a breath. "OK. Before I accept your... case, I'll need to know what happened. You'll need to tell me everything." I glanced through the open doorway that led into the dining room. No one looked unhappy about the lack of service yet.

"I can't tell you everything now. I don't have much time."

"So give me the *CliffsNotes*."

"I was arrested for breaking into and vandalizing Josie Carlson's bakery, The Little Cake Shop. Apparently, they found my glove there—it was specially embroidered, you see—but it's not mine because—" The line went dead.

"Hello? Miss Rogers?" I pulled the cellphone away from my ear and frowned at the screen. "Darn."

My interest was piqued. A mystery case about a break-in that involved the local bakery? Which just so happened to be run by one of my least favorite people in Gossip?

And when I'd just started getting bored with the push and pull of everyday life at the inn?

Count me in.

Want to read more? You can grab **the first book** in *the Gossip Cozy Mystery series* on all major retailers.

Happy reading, friend!

Paperbacks Available by Rosie A. Point

A Burger Bar Mystery series
The Fiesta Burger Murder

The Double Cheese Burger Murder

The Chicken Burger Murder

The Breakfast Burger Murder

The Salmon Burger Murder

The Cheesy Steak Burger Murder

A Bite-sized Bakery Cozy Mystery series
Murder by Chocolate

Marzipan and Murder

Creepy Cake Murder

Murder and Meringue Cake

Murder Under the Mistletoe

Murder Glazed Donuts

Choc Chip Murder

Macarons and Murder

Candy Cake Murder

Murder by Rainbow Cake

Murder With Sprinkles

Trick or Murder

Christmas Cake Murder

S'more Murder

Murder and Marshmallows

Donut Murder

Buttercream Murder

Chocolate Cherry Murder

Caramel Apple Murder

Red, White 'n Blue Murder

Pink Sprinkled Murder

Murder by Milkshake

Murder by Cupid Cake

Caramel Cupcake Murder

Cake Pops and Murder

A Milly Pepper Mystery series
Maple Drizzle Murder

A Sunny Side Up Cozy Mystery series
Murder Over Easy

Muffin But Murder

Chicken Murder Soup

Murderoni and Cheese

Lemon Murder Pie

A Gossip Cozy Mystery series
The Case of the Waffling Warrants

The Case of the Key Lime Crimes

The Case of the Custard Conspiracy

A Mission Inn-possible Cozy Mystery series
Vanilla Vendetta

Strawberry Sin

Cocoa Conviction

Mint Murder

Raspberry Revenge

Chocolate Chills

Made in the USA
Las Vegas, NV
12 February 2025

18028013R00104